*To the Archives Staff at
the Kansas State Historical Society*

The Jayhawker Cleveland

Also by David Hann

"The Deer on the Fence"
Living Now magazine, (from *River Memoir*)

"Sailors on a Sea of Grass"
Oskaloosa Independent (from *Sampling Kansas*)

"The Ballad of Jake Brakes"
Lawrence Journal World, Chanute Tribune, The Great American Poetry Show, Vol. 3, 2015

Sampling Kansas: A Guide to the Curious
Kansas Past: Pieces of the 34th, Star Penthe Press

River Memoir and Other Stories

The
Jayhawker
Cleveland

Phantom Horseman
of the Prairie

DAVID HANN

Anamcara Press LLC

Published in 2021 by Anamcara Press LLC
Author © 2021 by David Hann
Cover photograph courtesy of the Kansas State Historical Society, Topeka, Kansas.
Diana Dunkley, Tombstone Angel artist, Diana Dunkley at Studio 3D
Cover & Book design by Maureen Carroll
Adobe Caslon Pro, Tsisquilisda, Berlin Sans FB

Printed in the United States of America.

Book Description: David Hann shares the rich history of Bleeding Kansas and the Border Wars in The Jayhawker Cleveland. An historical tale of outlaws and heros. Hann takes the reader on a trail ride through a gritty time in the American West when people were pitted against each other and some had to choose sides in a life-and-death battle of ideas.

ANAMCARA PRESS LLC
P.O. Box 442072, Lawrence, KS 66044
https://anamcara-press.com/

Ordering Information:
Quantity sales. Special discounts are available on quantity purchases by corporations, associations, and others. For details, contact the publisher at the address above.
Orders by U.S. trade bookstores and wholesalers. Please contact Ingram Distribution.

ISBN-13: 978-1-941237-77-9 eBook
ISBN-13: 978-1-941237-78-6 hardback
ISBN-13: 978-1-941237-76-2 paperback

YAF069000   YOUNG ADULT FICTION / Westerns
YAF024160   YOUNG ADULT FICTION / Historical /
United States / Civil War Period (1850-1877)
BIO023000   BIOGRAPHY & AUTOBIOGRAPHY /
Adventurers & Explorers

Library of Congress Control Number: 2021940508

CONTENTS

PROLOGUE

CLEVELAND KILLED

The Leavenworth Herald, May 11, 1862

The Jayhawker Cleveland, alias Moore, alias Metz, killed at the Marais des Cygnes, by Lieut. Walker's men of the Sixth Kansas. His body was taken to Osawatomie. He had been in Kansas twelve months. Mustered in as a Captain in Jennison's regiment but was very soon mustered out.

He was a native of New York State, and his real name was Charles Metz. For a time he drove a stagecoach in Ohio. He had his first major brush with the law in Missouri and was sentenced to imprisonment in the state penitentiary, from which he escaped. Then he drifted west. Having assumed the name of Moore, he crossed the border to Kansas in the spring of 1861 and, perhaps as an echo of his life in Ohio, assumed the name of Cleveland.

Marshall Cleveland became popular as a fighting man at the time when Union men were so heartlessly driven from their homes in the border counties of Missouri and Kansas.

His "temporary wife" took him to St. Joseph and buried him, erecting to his memory the tombstone made famous by the caustic genius of John Ingalls. (Ingalls claimed that the tombstone carried an inscription, "One hero less on earth, one angel more in heaven" and on the reverse side was carved the figure of an angel holding a revolver in each hand.)

Chapter 1

NEW YORK CITY

Milo Metz swung his and Sarah's valises into the carriage. "We must hurry." Sarah gathered her shawl over a spreading belly to shield the soon-to-come baby from the July heat. She looked up into Milo's dark eyes, seeing the fear there, and pressed her face into his shoulder as he hugged her.

"See," Milo pointed. "Already, before dawn, even, everybody is getting out." People were filling the streets, afoot, on horseback or in carriages. All headed in the same direction, fleeing New York City, fleeing the cholera epidemic of 1832 that would kill more than 3,000 of the city's inhabitants.

"At least we have somewhere to go," said Sarah, "if we can get there."

"We'll get there, Sarah. Good old Asher Durand has a place for us in his country house in New Jersey. We've helped one another for years."

Milo hoisted Sarah into the carriage, seated himself, and charged off into the melee, lashing and cursing his horse and anything, horse or human that impeded their flight. Carriages and people, afoot and on horseback, struggled and pushed against one another in their flight from the city.

"Bear off!" shouted Milo, when another carriage attempted to cut in front of them.

"The hell with you!" came the reply, and the carriage driver waved a pistol towards Milo and Sarah.

"Your choice," Milo replied. Milo pulled his own pistol and shot the offender's horse, which crumpled, overturning its carriage. Milo urged his horse on, the driver's curses and the horse's screams soon drowned out in the melee.

"I'd be hanged for shooting a man," explained Milo in response to Sarah's horrified reaction. "Sorry about the horse."

As Milo and Sarah neared the steamboat landing the crowding increased in desperation and jostling. Panic drove people's actions as Milo forced his carriage through the throng. Finally, the buggies and carriages were too thick to push through. Milo stood up on the driver's seat and scanned the waterfront. He grinned, took off his cap and waved.

"One of Asher's boat crew," he said, "coming to get us."

Milo grabbed their bags and helped Sarah down. A young man dressed like a sailor ran up to them.

"Tim Olifant, sir. Crew for Mr. Asher Durand. Come along, please."

Milo noted Sarah's anxious look at their horse and carriage and gently guided her to follow Tim. "We can get another horse and carriage," said Milo. "We cannot get another life."

When Asher's private boat arrived with the Metzes at the country home on the Jersey Shore, Asher was there.

"Welcome," he said. "So glad you made it through the madness." Asher shook his head. "Poor devils who won't or can't get out. Who knows what will happen to them?"

"You are so kind," said Sarah. "It feels like the end of the world."

"We'll get through this, together," said Asher. As he spoke, a strikingly pretty woman arrived and took Sarah by the arm. "I'm Elizabeth Durand. Come with me and I will get you settled." Elizabeth and Sarah walked side by side up the gentle grassy slope to the Durand mansion.

Two footmen waited until greetings had finished, then at Asher's nod they picked up the Metzes' luggage and strode off toward the three-story columned house that overlooked the ocean. Asher clapped Milo on the shoulder and urged him to follow.

"What you need right now," Asher said, "is a stiff drink and I can use one also. I have excellent Tennessee whiskey. Come, my friend."

"I don't know how I can ever repay you for this," said Milo.

"I wouldn't have all this," gestured Asher, "if you hadn't taken a chance on my shipping business. My credit wasn't good enough to buy a rowboat, much less a ship, but you came through for me." Years at sea, first as an ordinary seaman, then working his way up to boson, first mate, captain, then owner of his own fleet of ships showed in Asher's lined face and strong build.

"I watched you work," said Milo, "and saw that all you needed was some support."

"And that you gave," said Asher. The two old friends strolled up to the mansion and sat on the porch. The butler approached and Asher held up two fingers in a V and said, "Two of Tennessee's best. Tall ones, and you may leave the bottle. Thank you, Phillip. This is my friend, Milo Metz."

Phillip bowed slightly. "I am at your service, sir." To Asher he said, "I anticipated a refresher would be in order." Moments later Phillip returned and poured a measure of Tennessee whiskey into each glass.

Asher raised his glass. "Here's for an end to the plague." Milo clinked his glass against Asher's. "And to New York rebuilding after this passes."

The New Yorkers happily accepted the summer sun and the slight ocean breeze that pushed away the heat. The Durands and the Metzes enjoyed one another's company, as they did of Dr. Robert Frank and his wife, Rosaline.

Horseback riding for Milo and Asher and croquet and buggy riding for the women. Reading or card games such as Binokel or Euchre filled out evenings. The Durands and their guests strolled around the estate, relieved to be out of New York but apprehensive about the future.

"Oh Milo," asked Sarah, "do you think we will be able to resume a normal life when we return to New York, if we return to New York?"

"Yes," Milo assured her. "When this is over, businesses will be eager to bounce back, and they will need our import and export services to distribute their wares, which will complement Asher's shipping business. We will help out one another as before this tragedy."

One day, slowly coursing back and forth in a swing beneath an apple tree, Sarah felt the baby coming.

Durand had offered a room in his sprawling country home to a doctor friend as well as to the Metzes and he chose well. Charles Metz entered the sunlit, peaceful world as a healthy baby.

By September the plague had run its course and the Durands and the Metzes with their newborn son returned to New York.

Milo's import and export business prospered, and Charles experienced a privileged life. He learned to ride and hunt and attended society events including the theatre, for which Charles found he had an aptitude, even joining thespians on stage in various roles.

"Charles is growing up to be quite the young man," said Milo, after the seventeen-year-old left to deliver some supplies to a customer.

"Yes," said Sarah. "He has learned to ride as well as you, and can handle our horse and buggy easily so you don't have to do the deliveries yourself."

"I don't know, though," said Milo, "if Charles is going to become a successful prosperous businessman or a successful and penniless actor."

"He does like the theatre," agreed Sarah, "and he likes to take in a play sometimes, even act occasionally, but I don't believe he would choose the theatre as a career."

"He likes applause," said Milo, "especially when it comes from young ladies. And Charles has a knack for acting. I never could get up on a stage in front of a bunch of people but it doesn't phase Charles."

"Do you think," asked Sarah, "that he can get into college?"

"Assuredly," said Milo. "Charles is smart and works hard and has that touch of ambition needed to succeed. We have enough connections to see that he has a decent chance for a good education."

The Cholera Epidemic of 1849 changed all that.

New York City's population had doubled to 500,000 people since the 1832 epidemic, but city leaders made no change in the sanitation system. Storm and sewer drains could not handle the ballooning population. The streets and alleys, messy before, doubled in the amount of waste that seeped into water supplies. Cholera killed more than 5,000 New Yorkers in 1849, among them, Milo and Sarah Metz.

If Charles's father hadn't gone out to deliver imported supplies to a local business, he might not have contracted the disease. Exhaustion from overwork weakened Milo's natural defenses. In just a few days, Milo's tall, muscular frame shed pounds and strength as the cholera worked its way through his body. Sarah, weak from worry about her husband and Charles, quickly succumbed also. Nausea and dysentery turned his once beautiful mother into a scarecrow of a woman. Charles didn't even have time to properly mourn the loss of his parents.

His mother's last words were, "Get out of this cursed city. Now. Save yourself. There is nothing you can do for us. Just see that we are buried together, then leave as quickly as you can."

Metz walked away from his parents' side-by-side graves in the Trinity churchyard. Just one week before, Charles and his parents were planning their own exit from New York, having purchased tickets on one of Cornelius Vanderbilt's steamboats plying the Hudson River.

"Mr. Metz?" came the query. "Mr. Charles Metz?" Charles had to stop his grieving to realize that now, "Mr. Metz" meant him.

"Yes," he replied, "that's me."

"Your father owes Kaspen and Company $500," said a well-suited man, flanked by a burly youth who looked like a street thug.

"I expect payment from Crossman's any day," said Charles. "I believe they may have had the sickness."

"The whole town's got the sickness," said the man, "but Mr. Kaspen doesn't care about that. He only cares about getting paid."

"I will speak with Mr. Crossman immediately," said Charles.

"Good. We'll be waiting. At your place. You better have something for us." The man fixed Charles with a glare, as did his companion. "This evening or else."

Charles knew that Crossman wouldn't pay, couldn't pay because he was dead, along with his family, but saying he would speak with Mr. Crossman bought Charles a bit of time. The Durand family had been hit hard by the cholera so there would be no help there with his debt problems. He still had three tickets for the steamboat he was to take with his parents. That is all he had. People who owed his father money had either died of the plague or fled town. Those creditors still in the city scrambled for money owed them while their debtors yet lived. Metz walked from the churchyard because debt-collectors had seized the family horse and carriage.

He knew that people were desperate to get steamboat tickets but his father's other creditors might be looking for him to board a boat. His funeral clothes stood out too much from the common crowd. He had to cover that up somehow. The stampede to leave town left debris in its wake. The heat of summer caused many people to jettison overcoats, even blankets. A stranger to the city could find the way to the docks just by following the trail of discarded clothing. Charles found a suitable cloak and threw that over his suit. Thus covered he slid along the road, collar turned up to hide his face. One hand clutched the cloak, another hand grasped a club. Milo Metz had often told Charles about their harrowing escape during the 1832 Cholera Epidemic. He would have preferred a revolver, but that lay at home, where no doubt Kaspen's thugs were waiting.

"Pardon me sir," Charles said to a couple with a child in tow. "Would you be wanting tickets? I don't need them anymore." Charles held out the tickets so the couple could see they were legitimate.

"How much?" came the suspicious reply.

"Same price I bought them for," said Charles. "My parents are dead now and I have nowhere to go."

"Oh, you poor boy," exclaimed the woman.

"You can have the means to get out of here," said Charles. "I suggest you take this chance to save yourself and your family. It's too late for me and mine."

The man studied the tickets and brought out a roll of bills for the exchange. The family dashed off towards the docks and Charles dashed off in the opposite direction.

Chapter 2

NEWARK, OHIO

Charles bought a seat on a stagecoach heading west, away from the cholera and away from his father's creditors looking for him to board a steamboat. Switching stagecoaches as he journeyed west, Charles arrived several days later in Newark, Licking County, Ohio. Riding on top of the coach most of the time because it was cheaper he chatted with the latest driver and that gave Charles an idea. Instead of getting off at the regular coach stop Charles rode with the driver to the stage livery. A large sign with two-foot letters proclaimed the place as Cutler's Livery and Delivery, with foot-high letters promising "Safe and Secure Passage for Person and Product."

"What happened, young man," said the driver, "fall asleep?" The driver looked to be about ten years older than seventeen-year-old Charles and was joking because it would have been impossible to sleep while riding on top of the pitching and rolling coach.

"No, sir," replied Charles. "I'm looking for a job. Could you use another hand here at the livery or on the coach?"

The driver regarded Charles, still wearing his formal funeral clothes, somewhat dusty from the long trip.

"What did you do?" asked the driver, "Run away and leave your bride at the altar?"

"I didn't leave some girl at the altar, but I did run away from some bill collectors seeking any money I had after the cholera killed my parents."

"That's tough," said the driver, who introduced himself as Bill Timmons. "I heard that the cholera killed several thousand in New York. Well, I've never had a passenger ask for a job and precious few ever called me sir," said the driver. "I've seen you are a respectable passenger at any rate. Let me talk with Mr. Cutler and see what he thinks. Have you had any experience handling horses?"

"Sure," said Charles, knowing that he could embroider his skill a little bit. "I've ridden as well as driven a buggy and was responsible for my father's team of horses." The reference to a team of horses was not true but Charles felt it was worth exaggerating his experience if that would land him a job.

Timmons came back a few minutes later.

"Mr. Cutler says a dollar a day and you can sleep in the stable until you've found a place to stay. The Irving Hotel serves breakfast and supper. Widow Irving charges fifty cents a day or ten dollars a month if you pay in advance."

Timmons saw the look on Charles's face and misinterpreted. "Sounds too good to be true," Timmons said. "Don't it?"

Charles was actually thinking of the nice apartment and lavish meals he enjoyed with his parents in New York. He never had to consider where the money came from to have all that, other than some vague notion that his father's business provided everything.

"Uhh," stammered Charles. "That sounds fine."

"Good," said Timmons. "I'll ask Mr. Cutler to put you on the payroll and when I come back I'll show you around."

Timmons returned and outlined to Charles what was expected of him. "Mucking stalls, rubbing down our stock when they come off a stage run, feeding and caring for all the other horses." Then he asked Charles to hold out his hands. Charles did so. Timmons gripped them and lightly squeezed. Miles of handling the reins of six-horse teams had produced in Timmons's shoulders and arms ripples of corded muscle. Years of sun and wind had bronzed and etched his face with lines, causing his eyes to shine like blue flame.

"Soft," said Timmons, "but your hands and the rest of you will toughen up. You may have noticed that we don't only board horses. We sell hay, grain, coal, and wood. You also see that we're located out here on the edge of town. I don't guess you've noticed the smell of manure and such, or if you did you were too nice or too smart to mention it."

"Oh, no," said Charles. "It's hard to separate horses from the manure." That remark set off a guffaw from Timmons. "You'll do, son."

Charles worked hard and had a knack for handling horses, including exercising horses of owners who paid for that service. Timmons watched him riding and said, "You ride like a cavalry trooper. You need to learn to shoot like one, better even, if you ever want to drive a stagecoach."

Several times a week Timmons instructed Charles in the proper handling of the cap-and-ball revolver. He saw that Charles already knew about shotguns from his hunting days before the cholera took everything away.

Charles kept at his work faithfully and noticed that more young females arranged to have their horses boarded at Cutler's Livery and Delivery. He inherited his father's height and strong but slender build, and his dark eyes and good looks moved people to trust him. Charles found he had an aptitude for horses and a gift for charming men and women. Timmons noticed the increase in female attention also.

"Seems like some of these young ladies have their eye on you," he said. "What are you now, twenty-one or so? Seems like you should be getting hitched pretty soon."

"I'm twenty-one," replied Charles. "I just try to be helpful to all our customers. A livery hand doesn't earn enough to support a wife, let alone a family."

"Just don't try to be too helpful to the young ladies," said Timmons. "I hear you've taken some of them out for buggy rides."

"Just showing them how it's done. Some girls these days want to handle their own transportation and I'm happy to help them learn."

"And I hear you are a genuine thespian, according to some of the young ladies."

"Well," said Charles, "I did take part in some stage performances in New York, including *The Gladiator*, where I played the part of Spartacus's son, under the great Edwin Forrest, and some Shakespeare plays which became more popular."

"Sure," said Timmons, "I know about Edwin Forrest and *The Gladiator*. That play hits too close to home for folks in the South and for folks who support slavery. The idea of slaves rising up against their owners, even in a play, has people calling *The Gladiator* an abolitionist play. If I was you I wouldn't mention *The Gladiator* when you talk about your acting experience."

"I understand," said Charles, "but Spartacus rose from a slave gladiator to a leader of slaves revolting against Rome. He was a hero."

"Well hell yes," said Timmons, "and the Romans killed

him. The best course for you is to keep your opinions to yourself. Even here in Ohio we have plenty of pro-slavers near the Kentucky border. Keep your mind on your work and stay out of trouble."

"I prefer Shakespeare, anyway" said Charles. "I don't intend to get involved, one way or the other. I will follow Polonius's advice to his son Laertes, 'Give thy thoughts no tongue'."

"Good advice," said Timmons. "I guess even I could learn a thing or two from that Brit."

A week or so after that talk, Timmons said, "The other driver, Henderson, gave notice that he wanted to try his luck prospecting in the California gold fields. I spoke with Mr. Cutler and recommended that you train as his replacement."

"Why, thank you, Mr. Timmons," said Charles. "I'll not disappoint you."

"Time you learned the real business of handling a team," said Timmons. "I've seen how well you do with taking care of our horses and getting them hitched up. You learn quickly and I'm getting to the point to where I wouldn't mind sharing my workload with a capable young man."

Timmons led Charles to the six-horse team and paused at the pair closest to the coach. "Now, we call these big boys the wheelers. They're the strongest, got the most pulling power and get these wheels moving." Timmons moved on. "These two in the middle we call the swing pair. They're really good at following the front two, what we call the leaders for obvious reasons. The leaders are always the most sure-footed and not prone to spooking."

"So it looks like," said Charles, "that not just any horse can be hitched up to a stagecoach."

"Right," said Timmons. "And not just anyone can be a stagecoach driver. Give me your hands."

Charles did so and Timmons gripped hard. "Now," said Timmons, "try to pull away." Charles pulled and Timmons pulled back, forcing Charles to come towards him. "Not bad," said Timmons. "See how all that hard work you've been doing has strengthened those arms and shoulders. You'll have six horses pulling the coach, and you have to be strong enough to control the reins but gentle enough so you don't injure or confuse the team. Never be rough with them. Stagecoach horses are expensive. It's almost as hard to get good stage horses as it is to find good drivers. Now, let's check the coach."

Timmons walked slowly around the coach. "This here coach is a Concord, finest coach there is." Timmons bent down to look under the coach and motioned Charles to do the same. He pointed to thick leather straps. "These," he said, "make the coach roll instead of bouncing, like it would do if it had springs. Makes the passengers a bit less uncomfortable."

Timmons carefully checked each wheel of the coach as they walked around it. "If you don't see someone grease the axles make sure you see it done or do it yourself. Check the spokes, too. If you lose a wheel you could turn over and there would be hell to pay."

Timmons continued his lecture as he inspected harnesses, reins, even the seats. "You may think this is being too careful, but you're going to be riding on there all day, and that small pebble or whatever is going to feel like a good-sized rock after a few miles. Let's climb aboard."

Timmons handed Charles a shotgun. "You told me you've hunted some, so if some road agent tries to hold us up, just you pretend he's a duck and let fly."

Timmons guided the coach away from the livery and stopped at the hotel. Charles noticed that Timmons occasionally leaned over towards one side and sometimes to the other. "Bet you don't know what I'm doing."

"You're right," said Charles. "What are you doing?"

"Okay now, listen carefully."

Charles did and he heard a faint ringing sound, which he reported to Timmons.

"That ring means the wheel is tight enough, and safe. If it was loose, you would've heard a kind of thudding sound, meaning it was starting to come loose. If that happens, make sure you get that wheel taken care of at the next station. You listen for that ring first thing as soon as the coach begins to move. You won't have leisure to lean over and listen once we get going."

"There's a lot more to stagecoaches than I thought," said Charles.

"Darn tootin'," said Timmons. "You'll learn. There's more learnin' that just has to come from doin'."

The two alighted from their positions when they stopped at the hotel. Charles helped the passengers with their baggage, stowing the larger items in the boot—a canvas-covered storage bin at the rear of the coach.

After helping the passengers board, Charles and Timmons climbed up to their seats. Timmons shook the reins, Charles grasped the shotgun, and the coach rumbled on.

That day's outing was uneventful—no unruly passengers, no holdup men, just a nice slow ride to station after station, changing horses as Timmons saw the need.

When he wasn't too tired and could afford a bath, Charles attended as many community events as he could, dressing according to a line in Hamlet, where Polonius advises his son Laertes about apparel. "Costly thy habit as thy purse can buy, But not express'd in fancy; rich, not gaudy; For the apparel oft proclaims the man."

Charles took note of what the upper crust in Newark wore and followed their dress as much as he could afford.

Even when stage driving he wore a frock coat and waist-coat. He noted that people treated him differently, with more respect and deference than when he wore his usual stall mucking and horse exercising clothes. Some people, including Timmons, called him Charlie, which he accepted while not liking the familiarity it implied.

Not all passages were as uneventful as Charles' first trip.

A mild wind stirred dust on a narrow dirt road flanked on either side by maples and oaks and scrub brush. A man on a gray horse pulled out of the trees cautiously. He cocked his head, listening, then clicked his booted heels against the side of his mount and moved onto the road. He removed his hat and mopped sweat from his face as he neared the top of a hill and carefully peered over the summit. Down the road six horses slowly pulled a bright red-painted stagecoach up the slope. The rider guided his horse into the trees on what would be the driver's side of the road. He pulled his revolver from its holster secured just in front of the saddle and checked the chambers. Satisfied, he returned the revolver to its holster and waited, waving an open hand in front of his face to disburse the gnats that gathered around his eyes. The late July morning was getting on to becoming a very warm day.

As the stagecoach drew closer he backed his mount farther into the brush. Timmons eased up on the six-horse team as the coach climbed the hill, chattering encouragement as they began pulling towards the summit. The man on horseback retrieved his revolver from its holster and tried to calm his nervousness with deep breaths.

The coach reached the top and the driver halted his team, allowing them to catch their breath after pulling the passenger-laden coach up the hill. The hidden rider clicked his heels against the horse's sides, cantered right in front of the team and waved his revolver.

The would-be robber yelled "Stand and deliv..."

Charles threw forward his shotgun and fired. The buckshot slammed into the robber's chest and he rolled off his mount, dropping his revolver when he hit the ground. The gray horse skittered into the road, stopped, then walked up to the other horses.

A female passenger screamed and male voices yelled to Timmons and Charles. "What happened? Are you all right?"

Timmons replied, "We're fine, but that fellow made his last attempted robbery. Charlie, I'll keep him covered and hold the team while you see to our fallen foe. How about you, Dr. Forsythe? Would you see if he's beyond help?"

A well-attired man, dark frock coat and Homburg hat, stepped from the coach and slowly walked towards the dying man. He stooped, put his hand to the man's throat to check for a pulse and shook his head. "The only help he needs now is prayers for his soul. He must not have known you two were driving this trip. How many does that make for you now, Charlie, two?"

"First one," he said. "I didn't shoot that other one after he turned his mount and fled."

"Two holdups you've foiled, Charlie," said the doctor.

Two men and two women stepped down from the coach. The younger man who was dressed like a drummer in checkered coat and waistcoat asked, "How come you didn't shoot the one you allowed to get away?"

"I figured he saw the error of his ways," said Charles. Timmons set the brake and Charles climbed down from his seat. He spoke softly to the gray, grabbed its reins and led it to where lay the dead holdup man. He stared at the bloody mess where the man's chest had been and turned away. He walked to the side of the road and vomited.

Timmons held up a canteen. "Rinse your mouth and

wash your face, then get help from some of the men to load him onto his horse."

Charles did as Timmons directed then threw the canteen to Timmons and called to those standing outside the coach. "A couple of you men help me hoist this fellow onto his mount. Maybe someone in Sharonville can identify him."

Taking care not to let blood drip onto clothes or boots, the male passengers set the dead man over the saddle of his horse while Charles held its muzzle. As Charles was tying the body onto the horse the youngest of the male passengers turned away and vomited. Charles motioned to Timmons for the canteen, which Timmons threw to Charles, who gave it to the young man. The drummer wiped his lips and sipped. "Thanks," he said. "I guess you're used to this sort of thing."

Charles shook his head. "I don't think I will ever get used to it," he said.

The passengers re-boarded the coach and Charles said to Timmons, "Sorry about losing it."

"Nothing to be ashamed of. It's not a pretty sight."

Charles led the gray to the rear of the coach and tied it to the boot, then climbed up to his seat. Timmons shook the reins and the team headed down the hill, with Timmons alternately using the brake to keep the coach from overtaking the horses. He glanced over to Charles and noticed his face was pale.

"Nasty business," said Timmons, "but it could have been one of us or a passenger headed to town slung over the back of a horse if you hadn't been quicker on the draw."

The news of the attempted holdup spread around Sharonville and to other stage stops. People in Newark thanked Charles for protecting the passengers. He noticed that some people were friendly but a little distant. The young women who had flirted with him were still interested in the handsome young man but most of them were hesitant. An exception was Becky Stuart, daughter of Newark banker Lancaster Stuart.

"My," she said, "I know that if I ride with you I will be safe." She tossed her blond hair and gazed at him with luminous blue eyes.

"I would like very much to have you ride with me," said Charles. "We could go for a buggy ride sometime. I've noticed you at the theatre performances when we have them. I very much like the theatre."

"That would be grand," she said, and Charles watched her blond curls dance as she strolled away.

Lancaster Stuart was one of the most prosperous men in Newark. Becky Stuart had many suitors eager for her hand and her father's money and influence—among them, Charles Metz.

"There are no proper suitors in this town for a young woman of your station," said Stuart.

"What about Charles Metz?"

I admit he has shown a great deal of drive and perseverance rising from a livery stable hand to a stagecoach driver, but what sort of family connections does he have?"

"Oh, father, you know that Charles's parents died in the Cholera Epidemic of 1849. He wasn't the only one in New York City who lost everything. Besides, he is so dashing, and a bit dangerous."

"Too dangerous for my liking. I won't forbid you to see him, but I can never agree to let you marry him."

"That's all right, father," said Becky. "He will do for now and the other girls envy me. I'm not ready for marriage, anyway, I don't think I could be happy living the rest of my life in Newark."

Charles continued to impress Mr. Timmons. After serving as guard and general assistant to Timmons for several years, Charles earned the position of alternate stage driver. A few years later, with the retirement of Mr. Timmons, Charles became the chief driver. The kindly Mr. Cutler had retired also, and sold his business to Rupert Sherman, who was not so kindly and was a bit more strict with his hired men. Sherman changed the name and motto of the stagecoach service from "Cutler's Livery and Delivery Safe and Secure Passage for Person and Product," to just "Sherman's Passengers and Freight." Had Charles been satisfied with being a horse groomer, or had taken on another occupation, his personal history and a portion of the Kansas-Missouri Border War history would have been different.

Chapter 3

LOCAL FAME

Smoke from cap-and-ball revolvers and rifled muskets joined clouds that drifted over Newark, Licking County, Ohio, in July 1860. A practiced ear could easily differentiate between the thwack of rifles and the sharper reports of revolvers as men participated in the shooting contest that was part of the Licking County July 4th celebration. Less than two years remained before many of the men gathered in a meadow below the clouds on that July afternoon would be surrounded by the noise and smoke of revolvers, muskets, rifles, cannons, and bursting shells. And the screams of wounded and dying men.

Battlefields had yet to be named and the great sorrow of a civil war with its hundreds of thousands of dead and wounded had yet to visit the citizens of the United States. Though united formally, the states and citizens within states already separated themselves according to their allegiance to the Union or to the cause of states' rights over that Union. States like Ohio, Kentucky, Tennessee, and Missouri were themselves split over the slavery issue and over loyalty to the Union versus loyalty to one's home state.

Charles Metz slid the four-pound .44 caliber Walker Colt up to eye level, sighted on the target briefly, and squeezed the trigger. The weight of the heavy revolver absorbed some of the recoil from the blast that kicked the barrel up… and as the barrel descended, Metz automatically cocked the hammer for a second shot, but this was only a shooting contest so he eased the hammer down while the onlookers cheered. The last shot had joined others in the bull's eye.

Townies wore the newly fashionable sack suits or the more common dark frock coat that Metz wore, and farmers or laborers wearing less formal attire cheered the popular Charles Metz, stagecoach driver and self-styled hero of numerous gun battles.

"You did it, Charlie. You did good for Newark!"

"What did you expect from the best shot in Licking County?"

The shooting contest judge said, "Congratulations, Mr. Metz, you win the prize money and this pair of Colt's revolvers." They were the Colt Navy Model 1851 .36 caliber revolvers, much lighter than the .44 Walker Colt revolvers which, given their size and weight, were generally carried in saddle holsters rather than worn at the waist. Metz wore his at his waist while driving the stagecoach.

"The best shot in Licking County and the best-dressed stagecoach driver in Ohio."

Women clustered together, at least as closely as the five to six-foot diameter hoopskirts allowed. Rigid steel cage crinolines held the skirts in a perfect circle. Newspaper caricatures of the day depicted bowing waiters reaching over the cloth and hoop divide worn by fashionable ladies, presenting appetizers and drinks on a long stick ending in a flat wooden plate that looked as though it could paddle a canoe if need be. Women also wore cape-like jackets without sleeves to cover shoulders while showing the fashionable wide sleeves, which completed the ensemble.

For sun and inclement weather protection, women of the day wore hooded cloaks, East Indian shawls or one woven in Paisley, Scotland; the town of Paisley in time becoming synonymous with its pattern that imitated Indian styles. Thus, it was a well-dressed crowd of townsfolk mingling with the simpler styles of tradesmen and farmers.

Metz, tall and lean, clean-shaven but for a mustache women found dashing, took in the praise with reserve. He smiled at the judge as he accepted the pair of Colts in their wooden case.

"Those Colts cost more than $13 apiece. And the $50 prize money isn't too shabby either."

"What's the prize for coming in second?" asked an onlooker.

"Funeral expenses, perhaps," said Metz. "Coming in second is sometimes fatal." In his years of stagecoach driving Metz had shot several would-be stagecoach robbers.

"Right you are, Charlie, spoken like a true guardian of the trail."

"He can guard me anytime," said one of the young women standing nearby. She regretted her outburst when she noticed the rolling eyes of her lady companions.

"Charlie's got plans too big for this burg," said a sympathetic friend. "Whoever heard of a stagecoach driver who dressed like a banker?"

"Or an actor," added someone else.

"Come on Charlie, give us some of that Shakespeare you're so fond of."

Metz blew out the cylinder of his still-warm dragoon pistol, and proceeded to load it, saying as he poured the black powder into a chamber and set the ball in place, "Once more into the breech, dear friends."

"Haw, haw, haw!"

"What a comic."

"Very clever," said the shooting contest judge, who was a judge of the county court as well. Judge Kramer guided Metz to the table set up for the town leaders. "A man who knows both Shakespeare and shooting is rare around these parts."

Metz walked up to the judge's table and accepted the winner's purse.

"Thank you, gentlemen."

"Well done, Mr. Metz. Our passengers and goods are safe when you drive the stage."

Metz nodded then turned from the table and his eyes swept across the crowd, acknowledging a wave here, a shout of congratulations there, still searching until he saw her.

Becky Stuart saw his glance, smiled demurely and turned to speak with a distinguished-looking older man, her father, a widower.

"It's all very well," said the older man, "to be friends with such a man, but he just isn't our sort, you know. You will find the right man back East, where you are going soon. Your mother's sister has the right connections for you and for the family. The Stuarts don't marry down."

"Oh, all right, father. Here he comes."

"Well then, I'll leave you two alone." Lancaster Stuart was made a bit uncomfortable when the stagecoach driver and pistoleer turned his gaze on him.

"Damned unnerving chap," the banker thought, "like he can read my mind and doesn't like what he sees, and he has shot a few men who tried to rob the stage."

Metz approached Becky as her father walked off.

"Oh Charles, congratulations!"

"Thank you, Becky." Then, noting Stuart's receding figure, he gestured with his chin.

"I wanted to chat with your father, too bad he had to leave."

"Yes, business, I'm afraid."

"He always seems to have business when I show up. I don't think he likes me much."

"Oh, don't be silly, it's just that father is so busy, what with the bank and the election approaching."

Charles looked into her eyes and his intense gaze softened.

"As long as you care about me, maybe your father will come around to liking me after awhile."

Becky looked down at her shoes and said, "I'll meet you at the barn dance tonight."

"Sure, that will be fine, although I would like to pick you up and convey you in style to the dance."

"Oh Charles, you haven't such a conveyance, and I don't want to walk like one of the common folk."

"I can get my boss, Sherman, to loan me his fancy buggy."

"If you can get Mr. Sherman to let go of his pride and joy I will gladly ride with you in style."

"Well, Mr. Sherman has to be out of town on business, so he won't mind at all."

"Pick me up at eight o'clock then. Bye."

Metz watched her walk off and mused that what Sherman didn't know wouldn't bother him. After all, Sherman entrusted Charles with his coach, horses, and passengers and their goods. Why not allow him to borrow his buggy for an evening? But Charles knew the answer because Sherman had already refused his request.

"No, Charles," Sherman had said. "I know you are a capable, trustworthy employee but as a matter of policy I don't loan anything to my employees."

"Well," thought Metz, "Some things are more important than a boss's trust."

Metz spent the remainder of the afternoon grooming Sherman's handsome Tennessee Walker, and then set about cleaning and polishing the fancy buggy. It was an Emerson, made in England, and had cost Sherman twice as much as one made in the States.

Metz remembered the black, gleaming buggy his father drove around New York City, remembered the pride in his mother's eyes when they rode through Central Park of an evening, and when they passed by his father's business. He also remembered the cholera, how it took his father's health, his business, then his mother, then his home, and along with his fortune, his friends.

The buggy, the horse, his father's and even his mother's clothes gone, sold for pennies. Well, he intended to rise from those ashes, be somebody, whatever it took. Driving a stage was just one more step in the ladder to financial and social success.

Becky was thrilled to see Charles drive up with the eye-catching horse and buggy. Metz thought to himself that Sherman would raise holy hell but the coming rebuke was worth the indignity if the impression of grandeur helped to win over Becky's father, and Becky's hand. Old man Stuart had just harrumphed, however, and turned back into the house after seeing off his daughter. Arriving at the dance, Becky saw the envious glances of her girlfriends, and noted their eyes admiring the handsome man as much as they did the splendid conveyance.

At the dance most of the talk centered around the slavery question. Licking County was squarely in the anti-slavery camp, but other parts of Ohio were not. Sentiments differed from town to town and one had to be careful when stating an opinion about the slavery issue.

"Old John Brown was a martyr to freedom's cause," said one man.

"More than a year passed since his raid on Harper's Ferry,'" said another, "and things haven't settled down a bit."

"Well, Brown decided to be a martyr and the government obliged."

"Much to their discredit. The hornet's nest has been stirred and there don't seem to be any chance of it unstirring."

"Not everyone thinks Brown was a martyr. There's plenty that sees him as a half-mad renegade."

Oregon's admittance into the Union in February 1859, had set the states evenly divided on the slavery issue. Kansas looked like it could go either way, depending upon which side could populate the territory and vote for their side.

"I tell you, men, that old Greeley was right, there's more persuasive power in a Sharp's rifle than a wagon load of your Bibles." Several pro-union men voiced their agreement.

"Besides, there's always some southern gospel sharp who can quote some scripture justifying slavery."

"It don't matter what the Bible says, slavery's not happening in Ohio."

"Whichever way Kansas goes will go the nation."

"And both sides are pouring into Kansas Territory to see their votes win."

"What about you, Charlie?" someone asked.

"Mr. Sherman has instructed his drivers not to get involved in politics," said Metz. He drifted away from the discussion and looked for Becky, whom he had left with some of her friends. Becky smiled at Charles as he approached. He nodded and smiled at the other young women and turned to Becky.

"Oh, thank God you are here," Becky said. "I must have some fresh air."

Charles extended his arm, which Becky took, and the two walked outside and along the grass edging the barn.

"Some people here think a war between the states is coming," he said.

"Oh, don't be silly," said Becky. "Whatever would they fight over?"

"Slavery is the big issue," he said, "with some calling for the abolition of slavery, by force if necessary."

"Oh, pooh," said Becky. "The Negro is happier here in the United States than back in Africa."

"Nat Turner and his followers didn't think so," said Charles.

"That was almost thirty years ago, ancient history," she replied.

"That ancient history was made more relevant by the success of *The Gladiator*, about Spartacus the gladiator-slave and his revolt against Rome."

"Which was rightly crushed by Rome," said Becky. "He didn't know when he was well off, and neither do the Negroes."

Charles saw that this conversation was heading onto dangerous ground so he changed the subject.

"Becky, are you and your father coming to our Thanksgiving Day presentation of *Henry the Fifth*?"

"Father isn't much interested in theatre. He says it is a waste of time and money."

"Well, I will be happy to see you there at any rate."

Becky glanced at Charles, then turned her head and looked ahead into the twilight and said nothing.

"Oh, it will be grand," said Charles. "I've always liked the character of Hal, the wastrel ne'er-do-well who becomes a king."

"But you're no ne'er-do-well. Everybody in town knows you showed up here without a cent, both parents lost to the cholera, yet worked your way up from horse-groomer to become the best and most reliable stagecoach driver around."

Becky stopped and smiled up at Charles.

"And, may I say, the handsomest and most accomplished thespian."

"I guess that's not enough of an accomplishment for your father to want to have anything to do with me."

"Father is just old-fashioned and he has old-fashioned ideas about social standing."

"And you, Becky, how do you feel about my social standing?"

"I'm with you now, aren't I? And didn't father permit you to take me to the dance?"

"Why, you are right. Do you think the old man, I mean, your father, might warm up to me someday?"

"I don't know, maybe. Anyway, let's not worry about the future right now."

Charles walked Becky back to the barn and the couple danced and talked with the other Licking County citizens, all come to celebrate a near perfect summer and promising harvest. But a shadow hung over the festivities. The growing animosity between the southern slave-owning states and the northern states, and their supporters within Ohio, could not be ignored.

Some Ohioans, traveling with free-staters, had already made the journey across the Ohio River, passing through Illinois and braving the dangers of Missouri to settle in Kansas and vote the free-state ticket. Charles supported the idea of equality for all men. Yet, he wasn't sure how far he was willing to go to back up his beliefs with action.

When Charles delivered Becky to her home, Lancaster Stuart waited at the doorway while Charles assisted Becky down from the buggy. He began to walk with her up to the house but Becky stopped him.

"I think it is best that we say our goodbye here."

"Of course, if that is what you think, but you meant good night, didn't you, not goodbye?"

"Oh, yes. Good night, Charles." Becky walked up the long path to the door, where her father waited.

Chapter 4

MR. SMITH AND
THE CONTRABANDS

Charles drove the buggy back to the livery stable, where Sherman kept his personal horses and buggies along with the animals and equipment used in his stage line business. He carefully groomed the horse, and cleaned and polished the buggy until it looked even better than when he had borrowed it. Then Charles went to bed, for he had to get up early to drive the morning stage.

A light rain fell during the night and the next day promised to be hot and steamy. Charles inspected the horses and their hitches, checked the coach for soundness and cleanliness, and checked his weapons, his two .44 dragoon pistols and shotgun. The new Colts Charles had won in the shooting match lay safely hidden beneath floorboards in his hotel room. No doubt the new pistols were superior to his much-used dragoons but Charles preferred to take weapons he had already relied upon. He would practice with the new Colts until, like the dragoons he had owned for years, his new Colts became like extensions of his hands.

The Ohio Stage Company had its most important stops in Cincinnati, Lebanon, Middleton, Eaton and Richmond, but the stage line had stations, or stages, along the route so that horses could be changed and passengers and drivers refreshed.

Charles had driven the route for several years and during that time repulsed several attempts by highwaymen to rob the stage. The robberies had ended badly for the highwaymen, who were either killed outright or fled not carrying gold and valuables taken from passengers, but rather lead from Metz's dragoons.

The trip would take three days, with stops at Sharonville, Lebanon, Middleton, and Eaton before ending the outward-bound passage at Richmond. Charles heard rumors about Sharonville being a stop on the Underground Railroad and was not surprised when a well-attired but tough-looking gentleman approached the stagecoach at Sharonville with a black couple and child. His light-gray suit and stylish Homburg hat suggested refinement and wealth. A tanned, lightly-lined face and wrinkles around eyes indicated a man who spent at least some time outdoors. Charles didn't ask, but the man, who said his name was Smith, identified the trio as his servants.

"I understand," said Smith, "that you are a trustworthy gentleman driver?"

Charles nodded in ascent and Smith put forth his hand as if to shake that of Charles, but his fingers held a gold coin. "Trustworthy and silent on certain matters?"

"Trustworthy and silent about your Othello and Desdemona and their progeny I assume." Charles pocketed the coin but saw the passengers would be crowded in the coach. "Why not have Othello sit up here with me to give the lady and child more room?"

Smith appeared to think over the offer while the couple exchanged worried glances.

"I like the fresh air," said Smith, and he climbed up to sit next to Charles. Charles noticed that Smith wore under his suit coat one of the new Navy Colts like he had won in the shooting match.

"Have you had much practice with your piece?"

Smith replied, "Yes, and some practical application as well."

Charles prompted the horses into motion and the stage moved out of Sharonville.

"I don't believe we will need any practical applications on this trip, but if I sit next to someone who is heeled I want him to know his business. I don't fancy getting shot by accident, or by intent, for that matter."

"I am truly heeled, as well as healed, sir," responded Smith, "for I once dealt in human chattel. Now I am making my amends, and must be heeled for that purpose."

"A good pun, Mr. Smith. You are a student of the Bard? Shakespeare dearly loved a pun."

"That I am, though my activities of late greatly limit such leisurely pursuits. And you sir, Mr. .....?"

"Metz, Charles Metz, and yes, when I can I read works of the great man."

Charles withdrew from an inside pocket a folded and worn document. "Lately I have been memorizing the part of Hal for our community presentation of *Henry V.* I practice if there is time when we stop to change horses. Now, however, I must attend to my other business, which is seeing this stage safely through to Eaton."

Smith said, "Yes, there are those who would seize my, my servants, and sell them like cattle."

"Risking your life to see them safely through is commendable. It appears that you have no compunction against risking my life also."

"I will take over the reins if you wish, and you may depart at will."

"No one takes over the reins when I am driving and no one takes what I carry. I protect the ill-gotten gains of the cardsharp as much as I do the hard-won savings of a farmer, and I protect anyone who rides on my stage."

The two men turned silent as the stage progressed along the road. Charles was gratified to see that Smith kept an alert eye on the surrounding terrain. The fact that there were few roads in that part of Ohio in 1860 presented advantages and disadvantages to criminals and law-abiding citizens alike.

The oaks, maples, and underbrush offered concealment but also hindered flight. The roads channeled potential victims along routes where robbers could plan to intercept travelers. However, people remembered who they encountered on the roads and strangers were usually noted, and suspected.

Local robbers preferred to attack near dusk, for they knew the ways through the brush. Criminals not familiar with the terrain preferred to attack earlier in the day to avoid getting lost making their getaway. The latter depended upon speed to elude pursuit, while the home-grown criminals adopted stealth and pre-selected hideaways. Charles related this to his companion.

"The slave catchers sometimes present a phony bill-of-sale too," said Smith, "and there are lawmen friendly to the slave cause who accept the bogus evidence and turn over those unfortunates to their captors."

Charles mused over this bit of information. "That would make matters a bit more complicated. I don't want to get into a shooting match with the law."

Smith kept looking around as the coach bounced and lurched over the road. "My guess is, first the slave catchers, if there are any, will try to bluff us, then maybe try force, and then try to find a friendly or bribable sheriff."

The first encounter took place at the Golden Lamb public house, in Lebanon, the next stop after Sharonville. Smith and Metz ate at the regular dining hall, while Smith's servants dined in the kitchen. Both men ate quickly and were finishing with coffee when Sally, a kitchen maid, stepped up to the table.

"You better come quick, Mr. Metz. Some men are bothering Mr. Smith's servants." This was not the first time that "servants" had visited the Golden Lamb, and most of the inn's staff were sympathetic to their plight and desire for freedom.

"Metz, I will go with Sally. You go around to the back."

Charles ran to the front door. Looking around he noticed a man holding six horses. Charles had not seen anyone enter through the front door of the Golden Lamb so he assumed the man was with at least two others and that the other three horses were for Smith's companions.

Charles knew the man would probably react with a warning cry if he ran around to the back so he paused at the door, rubbed his stomach, and stretched. He then walked slowly to the back as if intending to visit the outdoor privy, a not-uncommon practice for diners. The horse holder didn't take special notice as Charles walked around the corner. Once out of sight he pressed himself against the side of the tavern and glided to the back door, where he heard raised voices.

"Them darkies are contrabands and we mean to take 'em back to their rightful owner."

"Well gentlemen," Smith replied, "you are mistaken. I have had Isaac, Marie, and young Bartholomew under my employment for three years now."

"There's laws against helping escaped slaves. You could go to jail for this."

"As I said, gentlemen, these three are with me, where they will stay."

Charles stepped to the doorway, where he could see two men, armed but not presenting their pistols, and Smith, who stood between the two men and his three companions.

"Do you want to die for some escaped slaves? You look smarter than that."

Smith said, "I don't intend to die for my companions, but I will kill for them if need be." Charles saw that Smith had dropped his hand to the handle of his Colt.

"You can't win against both of us. Don't lose your life over these contrabands."

Charles drew a pistol and trained it on the backs of the two slave catchers. "You don't want to lose your life over these contrabands either, do you?"

The men turned to face Charles, and when they did so, Smith drew his piece.

"This ain't any of your affair, mister. Best you stay out of it," said one of the slave catchers.

"These people are all passengers on my stage, so it is my business. I usually don't pull out my pistol unless I shoot, so my finger is just naturally itching to squeeze the trigger."

"Just as mine is," said Smith, who had drawn his Colt.

The slave catchers whirled and saw they had been out-maneuvered. Charles stepped back, still covering them with his pistol and gestured with his free hand.

"Go back to your employer and tell him you followed a false trail."

"You haven't heard the last from us. We've got papers."

"Let's see 'em," said Smith.

"You'll see them in the hands of a sheriff."

Charles gestured toward the third man with the horses. "Until then, you'd best be on your way."

The slave catchers strode off to their horses, spoke briefly with the third man, mounted and rode off.

"Let's get going," said Charles.

Smith gathered his servants and watched them board the stage. No other riders had gotten on.

After Smith took his place next to Charles the coach started off.

"So, Mr. Smith, will the next encounter be through a sheriff or will they try force?"

"My guess is they will try to find a sympathetic sheriff," said Smith. I don't believe they want to get involved with stopping a stagecoach. Besides getting shot they could end up on the wrong side of the law."

"If they're serious about having the papers," said Charles, "we'll see them in Eaton or Richmond. If they had papers, why didn't they show them?"

"Maybe they knew I would have put them down the privy."

"Why Mr. Smith, you are a devious rascal."

"All in a good cause. Entire wars are fought for good causes and there are plenty of laws broken, God and human, in the course of a war. And, no mistake, we are going to be in a war of some kind before long."

"A genuine shooting war?" asked Charles. "Who with?"

"Against men like we saw today. I believe they would have tried force if you hadn't showed up."

"That would have led to painful consequences for them. No one bothers my passengers or cargo. I suspect your contrabands are a little of both."

"You've thrown in your lot with them and me now, and that gang won't forget."

The coach rolled through the hills, descended, and passed through a covered bridge. Charles and Smith kept especially alert, but there was no ambush. They did startle a young man and woman who had been resting, Smith remarked. Charles smiled.

"They call these covered bridges 'Kissing Bridges' and I suspect the name is apt for those two." The couple started to walk quickly up a trail, but the young man turned when Charles hailed him.

"Good morning. Have you by chance seen three men riding through, leading three horses?"

"We sure did. They almost ran us down. They seemed to be in an awful hurry."

Charles thanked them and urged on the horses.

"We have one more covered bridge before we get to Eaton, so we're not out of the woods yet."

Smith gazed at the surrounding trees.

"Looks like we will be in the woods for a spell."

"That's right, so it will be prudent to keep alert. Your friends may be heading straight for Richmond or they may be scouting likely places to waylay us."

"Either way," Smith said, "I don't plan on surrendering my charges to the likes of those scum."

"Have you ever killed a man?"

"Best not to ask that question," said Smith. "Some men are likely to say they have, just to appear dangerous, and some men are likely to say they haven't, so they don't appear as dangerous as they really are."

"Well, you carry your sidearm like it seems natural."

"Observation without questions is the best teacher, as far as guns are concerned. A man doesn't always want to talk about his past and it is best not to ask. That advice is more important to follow the farther west one travels."

The coach pulled up a long sloping hill, not steep, but one of those hills that deceive walker or horseman into maintaining the same pace used over level ground. Charles had been over the route many times and knew better than to wind his horses by pushing them too hard.

"Down from this hill is the last covered bridge before we get to Eaton. I expect that is where your friends will try to intercept us, if they plan to use force."

Smith asked, "So, how do you want to play this?"

"I figure the gang will be waiting inside. I plan to smoke them out while you stay with the coach."

"Better yet," said Smith, "I'll smoke them out while you stay with the coach. You know how to handle the team and if I'm not mistaken, you know how to fight from your perch there."

The stagecoach eased down the hill nearing the covered bridge, which lay in shadows cast by the surrounding hills. Charles continued his slow approach to the structure, then stopped when he was several hundred yards off and went through the motions of inspecting the coach wheels and team harness. Smith slipped off the coach and made his way stealthily through the trees and brush to the covered bridge. Smith had the shotgun in one hand and the holstered Colt at his side.

Charles leaned into the window of the coach.

"When I get moving, you folks get down low as you can. There may be shooting up ahead. Don't look up to see what is happening."

The father, Isaac, said nothing but Charles felt the man wanted to do something other than be a passive passenger. Charles handed one of his dragoons to the man, who grimaced as he accepted it. "Don't shoot unless you have to."

Marie said, "You and Mr. Smith are angels."

Isaac added, "Yes, but they are angels with flaming swords, come to drive those evil men from Eden."

Charles laughed. "Ohio isn't exactly Eden, but we'll try to make Ohio plenty hot for them anyway. Remember, stay down and don't shoot unless you must."

Charles ascended to his seat and waited for the action to begin.

Smith's shotgun boomed.

"Gotcha, you lily-livered trash!"

The far side of the covered bridge erupted in a flurry of horses, men clinging to their necks and keeping low while Smith fired another shotgun round over their heads. Just for good measure, Smith pulled his Colt and let loose a couple of rounds skyward. The three men spurred their horses onward while Charles leisurely brought up the coach.

"Well done, Mr. Smith, even if you didn't hit any of them."

"Oh, that would have just complicated things. We'd have to take care of a wounded man and we would sure have to explain a dead one."

"I guess this means the next attempt will be through legal means," said Metz, "but I imagine you have had some experience along those lines."

"Yes, we'll just have to see how things go in Eaton or Richmond. I don't think that bunch will try another ambuscade. They may fear, rightly so, that my patience with them is running out."

Charles gestured toward the dragoon he had given Isaac.

"As it happens, I just came into possession of two new Colt's revolvers. When we part company I'll give you some powder, caps, and balls. I am sure Mr. Smith can instruct you in their use."

"You should keep it," said Isaac, pushing the pistol back to Metz. "He who lives by the sword dies by the sword."

Charles took the dragoon and holstered it.

"Trouble is plenty of people die by the sword, or guns, who never held one. I would rather have a choice in how I go."

Smith looked at Charles, appraising him.

"I believe you. I hope one day to put away my guns and practice law, but I think you just naturally take to using a gun."

"Natural or not, it's my trade right now."

"Just try to stay on the right side of the law," said Smith.

"I'll just stay on the side I think is right, and let the law fall on either side of me," said Metz. "You know the law has a way of changing with the times. It's illegal to help slaves escape their bondage, even here in Ohio, but that hasn't stopped you, has it?"

Smith nodded his head, agreeing. "What's right isn't necessarily what's lawful."

Charles started the horses and proceeded up the road to Eaton, where he would stable his horses and Smith could get accommodations for his three charges. Charles didn't need to prod the horses because they knew from previous trips that they would be relieved of their load soon.

Smith noted the eagerness of the team.

"Those horses act like they have business to attend to in town."

"Yes, and I bet they can find their way to the livery stable without my help. That is where I'll unhitch them and we all can take a break before finishing up this trip at Richmond. We'll stay overnight here. I've got mail to take to Dan Reid, the postmaster here. I'm not certain what kind of welcoming committee there might be for your, ahem, servants."

"I have my own connections, thank you," said Smith. "You may not know this, being a man not interested in politics, but some people in Ohio have been fighting slavery since 1816. Eaton has been one of the safest towns in the state for those fleeing bondage."

Ohio was fragmented by counties that opposed slavery and counties that supported slavery. Smith was right about Eaton being a safe town and the stagecoach stopped long enough to rest and water the team and allow everyone to stretch their legs before resuming the journey to Richmond. Smith and his companions stayed close to the coach.

"Don't worry, my friends," Smith assured the fugitive slave family. "We'll be passing on at Richmond and join up with other right-thinking folks who will see you safe on your way North, and freedom."

Smith was right about joining up with other right-thinking folks, except that union didn't occur the way he had planned.

Chapter 5

JAILED AND FIRED

Mr. Smith was right about the slave catchers fore-going the use of force and trying a friendly law-man. When the coach arrived in Richmond the next day, Charles and Smith saw the slave catchers. Standing next to them was the sheriff.

"That's them what pulled their pistols on us!" shouted one of the slave catchers. "Arrest 'em, sheriff!"

"They wouldn't, or couldn't, show any papers," said Smith.

"Well," said the sheriff, "Mr. Shaw and Mr. Adams just showed them to me and the papers look to be in order." The sheriff's face hardened, "Hand 'em over."

To Metz's surprise, Smith didn't protest.

"Okay sheriff, I don't want to break the law."

Isaac, Mary, and Bartholomew stepped out of the coach. Isaac's face was impassive, Mary was crying and the boy looked frightened.

The sheriff relaxed. Smith appeared to take the defeat with nonchalance.

"I'd like a judge to approve this," said Smith.

"I'm the one who decides what a judge sees," said the sheriff, "and these three runaways are going with these deputies after they spend a night in jail."

"Deputies!" Metz exclaimed. "They're just road agents. They were all set to ambush this coach back down the road."

The sheriff looked up at Metz. "You best stay out of this, driver, 'lest you want to go to jail. That'd cost you your job, sure."

"It's okay, Metz," said Smith. "Sometimes one has to admit defeat."

"Then if it's all right with you, sheriff," said Metz, "I'll just get the team to the livery stable and get a room for the night. The stage heads back first thing in the morning. I have to check with the stage depot to see if we have any passengers."

Smith joined Metz in the hotel dining room. Metz nodded at Smith and continued eating.

"I'm sorry you lost your cargo."

Smith ordered his meal and sat back in his chair. "Oh, it's not a permanent loss. Isaac and family are safer where they are now than if they were in the hands of the slave catchers."

"So, what will your move be now?"

"Well, Metz, you probably know that not every town has a sheriff like this one, or citizens like the ones in this town, for that matter."

"I don't understand."

"It is better that you don't understand. You should just get a good night's sleep and head back to Newark."

"That I intend to do." Metz rose from his chair and headed for his room.

"Remember what I said," advised Smith. "Get a good night's sleep, and if you hear a ruckus just stay in your room."

"No problem with that. I hope to sleep soundly 'till dawn. I've paid my bill in advance and asked the desk clerk to rouse me at first light."

Metz did sleep soundly until dawn, not knowing that Smith rode to Lebanon, gathered townspeople and students and faculty from nearby Oberlin College, forty of them, and set out for the Richmond jail to release the family from captivity. The liberators manhandled the sheriff a bit and locked him in his own jail.

The knock on Metz's door came not from the desk clerk, but from an irate sheriff.

"I've got one of you contraband thieves at least. Now get dressed and get over to the jail."

"What is this all about, sheriff?"

"Don't play dumb with me, stagecoach driver. You're in this up to your neck."

Metz's protests were to no avail.

When the sheriff led Metz downstairs, Metz yelled over to the desk.

"Hey, clerk, tell him I didn't go out last night."

"That's right, sheriff, this man was up to his room all night as far as I know."

"Well, maybe you don't know all there is to know, young feller. You stay out of this."

The sheriff led Metz to the jail and locked him in.

"You'll just stay here until we round up the rest of those slave-stealers. I've telegraphed to Senator Langhorn's office. He'll get in touch with President Buchanan and he knows how to handle slave-stealers."

Within the week, President Buchanan ordered the U.S. Army to pursue and arrest the "Liberators," or "Rescuers," as they were dubbed in the press. Metz and the Lebanon and Eaton citizens who rescued the family became known, not always sympathetically, as "The Liberators" and were prosecuted, and eventually tried and convicted by an all-Democrat jury. The group ultimately bargained with the prosecutors, who granted the group their freedom in exchange for the promise that they would stay out of Richmond.

Metz received two letters while waiting to be tried along with the Libertors. The first letter was from Becky, addressed "In care of the Richmond jail." The letter began with, "Charles," not "Dear Charlie," or "My Dear Charles," and that beginning set off a sinking sensation in Metz's stomach. It read:

> *I was sorry to learn that you have stooped to outlawry. I don't know how much you were paid to rough up and embarrass my father's good friend, Sheriff Martin, but now that I have seen your true stripes, it doesn't matter. I am mortified and embarrassed to be associated with a criminal. As you are reading this letter, I am traveling east, not to return. My father said he will have you arrested if you try to follow me. Goodbye. Becky Stuart.*

The second letter came from Mr. Sherman.

> *Due to your legal entanglements I have had to send another driver to continue your route. Your actions with the band of marauders leaves me with no choice but to dismiss you immediately. Rupert Sherman*

Learning that Metz was fired, Sheriff Martin laughed at Metz's plight. His pride was still stung after being locked up in his own jail.

"You won't have much chance for a career as a stage-coach driver in Ohio if you can't go certain places in the state. Maybe you should try looking for a job out west."

Metz was released along with the Liberators. The mysterious Mr. Smith was never apprehended. Another driver had taken the stagecoach to complete its route so Metz had to wait for another ride. When Metz returned to Newark, after riding in disgrace atop the coach, he went right to Mr. Sherman's office.

"I've come for my pay."

"You didn't complete your route."

"You'll pay me for what I did complete."

Sherman tried to stare him down but couldn't stand up to Metz's intense eyes boring into his. Sherman noticed that Metz was wearing his Colt's revolvers, his hands crossed in front of his belt, hands too close to the weapons that had drawn blood many times. Sherman sighed, opened his desk drawer, and retrieved several bills.

"Take it and get out. You're through around here, Metz."

Metz counted the money and stuffed it into his inside coat pocket.

"Thou art a varlet, a knave, a prig, a coxcomb."

Metz strode out of Sherman's office leaving him puzzling over Metz's parting words.

Chapter 6

THE CALIFORNIA CONGRESS

After settling his bill with the hotel, Charles stood outside, pondering his next move, knowing that he would have to leave Newark, and the state of Ohio. A man who looked like a preacher or a college professor approached Metz.

"You're Metz, aren't you, the stagecoach driver?"

"Former stagecoach driver."

"Looking for work?"

"Maybe. Depends."

"I speak for the California Congress, twenty good souls bound for Kansas, Mr. Metz. We could use someone who has experience handling road agents. Doesn't hurt that you know horses, as well."

"Wait," said Metz. "You call yourselves the California Congress but you're intending to settle in Kansas?"

"We most likely wouldn't get very far if we called ourselves the Kansas Congress, would we?"

"Tell me more, mister...?"

"I am the Reverend Alistair Stansider, elected leader of this band. We're pledging our votes, our fortunes, our very lives to vote Kansas a free state."

"From what I've heard about that part of the country you might lose your fortunes and your lives as well as your votes before you reach Kansas."

"That," replied Stansider, "is why we need someone like you. We've heard the stories, how free staters have to run a gauntlet of slave staters through Missouri." Stansider gestured to the revolvers Metz wore. "And we've heard how handy you are with pistol and shotgun."

"I'm no gunman," protested Metz. "I've only used my weapons when I needed to."

"We've heard that, too," said Stansider. "We don't want someone who is too ready to use violence. It may be enough to just show whomever we meet that we can defend ourselves."

"I've had dealings with their lot," said Metz, "I and my companions were able to avoid violence, but it was a close thing. Why don't you get to Kansas by riverboat instead of chancing an overland route?"

"The word is," said Stansider, "that people traveling along the Missouri River are subject to interrogation at any point where the boat stops, and a wrong answer means we lose everything we have, maybe our lives as well. I doubt if we would be as lucky as the Cincinnati Company was on the Hartford."

In 1855 the riverboat Hartford had steamed 390 miles down the Ohio River to Cincinnati, where the settlers, calling themselves the Cincinnati Company, boarded. They rolled another 390 miles to the Ohio River's junction with the Mississippi River at Cairo, Illinois, 160 miles up the Mississippi to St. Louis, Missouri, which was the junction of the Mississippi and the Missouri rivers. Pro-slavery officials in Missouri suspected (correctly) that the passengers were free staters and delayed the Hartford for several days in St. Louis before allowing its departure.

The Hartford's stern-wheel paddles churned 310 miles westward to Kansas City, then 110 miles up the Kaw River, where the steamboat ran aground near the junction of the Smoky Hill and Republican rivers. The Cincinnati Company named their town Manhattan.

The California Congress, encouraged by the successful emigration of free state settlers on the Hartford five years before, decided they would bolster the free state movement in Kansas, but didn't understand the brutal nature of the free state-slave state issue.

While free staters were coming into Kansas from Ohio, Illinois, and the Northeast, slave staters entered Kansas from the southern pro-slavery states and from Missouri. Both Kansas and Missouri seethed with conflict. Free state Missourians found themselves threatened, evicted, or killed by slave state Missourians. Anti-slavery Missourians fled to Kansas, where they received the same treatment from slave staters who raided into Kansas. Free state Kansans, some of whom had been driven from Missouri, attacked slave staters in Kansas and crossed into Missouri to wreck revenge. Missourians, including former Kansas slave staters crossed into Kansas, seeking their own revenge. Thus, the term, "Bleeding Kansas," could have been applied to Missouri as well as to Kansas.

Into this conflict came the California Congress, and Charles Metz. Waiting to prey on such settlers were McCabe, Shaw, and Adams, the would-be slave catchers foiled by Mr. Smith and Metz. They preceded the California Congress by weeks. Missouri and Kansas looked like fertile ground for slave-catching, and there were free staters to waylay and plunder.

The trio had nothing to return to in their home state of Alabama. Their families were sharecroppers and these sons of Alabama had never taken to working the land. The local sheriff had strongly insisted that the three find something to do, no matter what it was, as long as they didn't do it in Alabama. No family member missed them because the little work they did was more than offset by the cost and trouble of their room and board. At least their families could boast that their sons had gone west to fight for the South.

The sons of Alabama had done more plundering than fighting. The money and goods taken from settlers went into new clothes and good horses.

"Hey now," said McCabe to Shaw and Adams. "Don't we look like real life desperadoes?"

Shaw doffed his hat with its rattlesnake headband and wild turkey plume, and held it out for them to see. "I'm a genyoowine Alabama hell raiser." He held his arms out to the side to show off the long fringes of his buckskin jacket.

Adams elected to dress all in black, believing that made him look more sinister. "And me," said Adams, "I'm the Angel of Death to abolitionists. See here," as he held up his black hat with an Ace of Spades stuck in the hatband. "When they see me they'll think Judgement Day is come, for sure."

McCabe wore a wild turkey plume in his hatband. His hatband was a cartridge belt filled with bullets and he had both sides of his hat turned up. "Those abolitionist sons-of-bitches will know I mean business when they see me." McCabe rubbed his neck and rolled his head. "Them heavy bullets make my neck a mite sore, though."

"Yeah," said Shaw. "Maybe you should shed some of them bullets and just leave three for the front part of your chapeau."

"Chapeau, is it?" replied McCabe, suddenly angry. "Who are you calling a chapeau?"

"No, no," said Shaw. "A chapeau is just a Frenchy word for hat. No need to get riled."

McCabe calmed down then and unloaded several bullets from his hatband. He re-set his chapeau and twisted his head around several times. "That is an improvement, I must confess."

"Enough of this chitchat," said Adams. "I want to pile into some of them abolitionists."

The men's surly and domineering manners intimidated most free staters and their families, who were farmers or businessmen, not gunmen. They haunted the trails leading to Kansas. Their favorite and most fruitful quarry were settlers with families, like the California Congress.

Metz found that his settlers knew enough about horses that he did not need to instruct them along those lines. Most of the men in the California Congress had hunted and were not strangers to firearms; however, they had hunted animals, not men.

"I'd like to see your weapons," said Metz.

The settlers were surprised at the request but complied.

"So it seems," Metz continued, "that you have plenty muskets, some rifled muskets, and shotguns. Don't any of you have a handgun?"

The California Congress settlers produced a dozen handguns, four muzzle-loading muskets and six of Walker's 1851 Colts, the same revolvers that Metz carried, and two other revolvers of dubious manufacture and quality.

"At least you have kept your weapons clean," said Metz. "I just wish you had more. You all have read the newspapers and should know that we're headed into dangerous territory."

"We're not heading to Kansas to start a fight," said Stansider. "We intend to settle there and vote free state."

"The fight's been going on since 1854," said Metz. "I don't think you will be able to avoid fighting, if only to defend yourselves."

Most of the company rebelled at the thought of shooting their fellow men. Bibles flourished. "Vengeance is Mine, saith the Lord. Who lives by the sword dies by the sword."

Metz tried persuasion and common sense.

"The slave staters are not your fellow men and they won't hesitate to shoot you, and self-defense is not vengeance," argued Metz. "I have mentioned this before to people with the same sentiments as you. Many die by the sword, or gun, who never held one in their hands."

Metz also found that the settlers were very slow when it came to loading their weapons. They were accustomed to only loading their weapons when preparing to hunt. Some of the revolver owners had never loaded their weapons, apparently keeping them only for show.

"Too slow," said Metz, "too slow. If brigands show up, as I am sure they will, they will be upon you before you are ready to defend yourselves. What do you think will happen to your womenfolk after you men are killed?"

"Won't they see that we mean no harm?" asked one settler.

"Oh, yes," said Metz. "They will see that you mean no harm, just like the quail or ducks or deer you shoot mean you no harm. They will shoot you down with the same compassion you show to the game you hunt. You are the game they hunt."

The California Congress grumbled about the frequent inspections of weapons and loading drills insisted on by Metz but they knew as well as Metz the stories of outrages committed against free staters.

Metz was not surprised when the California Congress settlers did not show their guns at the approach of three riders who appeared while the group was almost ready to cross into Missouri.

McCabe, Shaw, and Adams rode hard up to the wagon train. They had learned that an aggressive approach often led to meek cooperation from their victims. All wore revolvers and Adams carried a shotgun as well.

"We don't want trouble," said Stansider.

"Well," growled McCabe, "trouble is what you got."

Metz had ridden off and now approached the slave catchers cum bushwhackers from the side. He did this partly for surprise, partly so he would not draw fire toward the settlers, and partly because he didn't want to get between the settlers and the brigands and risk getting shot by mistake in case his own party did put up a fight. Metz rode up with one of his .44s leveled at the trio.

"I've got trouble enough for the likes of you."

"He's bluffing," said Shaw, who put his hand on his pistol. Adams started to swing his shotgun around and Metz's Colt boomed, the .44 slug blew Adams from his saddle. Shaw stopped his draw. He and McCabe held up their hands. Some women screamed.

"Git," said Metz, and McCabe and Shaw started to wheel their horses around. "No, wait," he added. "Take this carrion with you. Get down off your horses and tie your friend over his saddle. This is the last time I will spare your lives."

Stansider looked up at Metz from his seat at the head of the wagon train as McCabe and Shaw rode off with their dead friend.

"You just shot that man. They didn't fire a shot."

Another man said, "You didn't give them a chance."

"They had a chance not to try to shoot me. Besides, I've run into them before, back in Ohio, and I didn't shoot them then. I let them live. They didn't learn."

That night the California Congress settlers were cool to Metz.

"You've seen what lies ahead of you," Metz said. "Do you want to go on, and more to the point, do you want me to go on with you?"

The settlers looked west into the darkness that was Missouri.

"No, no, we need you. We just don't want anyone killed."

"I don't either," said Metz, "especially me. In the days to come you will have to choose between fighting and dying, or at the least between fighting or being robbed by bushwhackers."

"I've hunted some, and I'm willing to fight, but I don't know anything about fighting with the likes of those three gunmen." This came from young Allen French.

"I'm willing to fight, too," said Homer Perry.

"Me too," said Stanley Mead. "I'm willing to learn how to defend myself and others who can't fight."

They were all young men, just a few years younger than Metz.

"All right," said Metz, "You'll begin practicing when we stop for the night."

In the days that followed, Metz instructed the three men in all aspects of the cap-and-ball revolver and the Sharps rifle. He taught them how to melt and mold lead so they could make their own ammunition, how to take care of their weapons, how to shoot, and how to treat wounds caused by those weapons.

"But the real challenge you will face," Metz said, "is when you have to decide whether or not to pull the trigger on someone. And you better make up your mind that you will do so because your opponent has already made up his mind to shoot you and most likely has already shot and killed men."

Allen French hefted his Walker Colt. "I'm not letting anyone bully me without a fight." "Same goes for me," said

Stanley Mead, and Homer Perry grasped his revolver and rotated the six cylinders. "We've got to learn," he said, "and fight if we must."

The young men practiced every night and during the day when travel was halted. Metz had them throw their pistols and rifles to one another, pick up a pistol from the ground and go through the motions of firing. He told them that if they only carried one revolver they should get extra cylinders that would fit their revolver so they could hurriedly reload. He persuaded his pupils to carry their revolvers with them at all times so they would get used to their weight and get used to knowing they should be ready at any time to defend themselves and their companions.

The six hundred-plus miles of travel from Licking County at the rate of maybe two miles per hour, plus inevitable delays from breakdowns and river crossings brought the California Congress into Putnam County, Missouri in late August. There wasn't any point in trying to disguise their eastward origins. Metz kept alert for more highwaymen and told the California Congress settlers to carry their firearms openly so that observers would know this company of travelers was armed. Metz knew that the settlers, with the exception of the few he had trained, would not put up a fight and would be no match for experienced gunmen. He hoped the display of guns along with the story of his killing one highwayman would ward off the less enthusiastic trouble-makers.

McCabe and Shaw found a friendly sheriff in the first town they came to and warned him that a gang of abolitionists was coming with the aim of settling in Kansas, led by a man who participated in the liberation of the runaways in Ohio and who had killed their friend. The sheriff rode out and intercepted the settlers.

"Man name of Metz with this party?" asked the sheriff.

"That's me," said Metz.

"I got a dead man brought into town. Two men say you killed him in cold blood."

Metz gestured toward the settlers. "They can vouch for me defending myself and them from those highwaymen." Choruses of "That's right, sheriff" followed Metz's words. The sheriff placed his hands on the pommel of his saddle and leaned towards Metz.

"You'll have a chance to convince a judge of that. You're coming with me to stand trial for murder."

Metz felt he had no choice but to go with the sheriff.

"Some of you will have to come along," said the sheriff, "as witnesses."

Stansider and a few other settlers agreed to come with the sheriff.

"We're only heading out to California," said Stansider. "We're not looking for any trouble."

"That's right, sheriff," said Homer Perry. "We plan to stop off at Westport for supplies before heading farther west. We don't have any intention to disturb anyone in Missouri."

"You can tell all that to the judge," said the sheriff. "And Mr. Metz here will have a chance to tell his side, too."

Chapter 7

MISSOURI LAW

D amn slave-stealing trash," one deputy snarled when
he threw Metz into a cell.

"I hope you hang," said another deputy.

When time came for the trial, the deputies dragged
Metz from his cot onto the floor of his cell, not giving him
a chance to get up and walk. They rolled him on the dirty
floor, wrinkling his dark frock suit and scuffing his polished boots. Each gripped an arm as they led Metz into
the courtroom. "Just hope you two don't meet up with me
again," said Metz.

Minutes later, Charles Metz sweated in the humid heat
of August 1860 as he stood before Judge Francis McCall.
Weeks on the trail looking after the California Congress
settlers had thinned his tall frame but his eyes were still
black and piercing. Metz managed to comb his dark hair
and mustache.

The judge banged his gavel.

"You appear before this court facing two serious charges,
murder and slave-stealing. Let's handle these charges one
at a time. How do you plead, Mr. Metz to the charge of
murder?"

"Not guilty, your honor, by reason of self-defense."

"I have listened to the testimony of the California Congress settlers and to the testimony of Mr. McCabe and Mr. Shaw, friends of the deceased."

Judge McCall glared at McCabe and Shaw.

"Seems like you boys rode up to this party of settlers with malice aforethought. It is plain from the testimony here that Mr. Metz was defending himself and his companions. When the unfortunate Mr. Adams swung his shotgun around, a fair-minded person would have thought he intended to discharge said shotgun." Judge McCall banged his gavel.

"Not guilty, by reason of self-defense."

Metz relaxed, but not for long as the judge continued, "However, young man, you aren't out of the woods yet, not by a long shot. This court don't abide with outlawry. By that, I mean your reputation has preceded you. That is, you are a no-good slave-stealing abolitionist."

The Judge held up a piece of paper and shook it.

"This here wire confirms that you were one of those miscreants, the so-called Liberators or Rescuers, who broke into Sheriff Martin's office back in Jefferson County, Ohio. That party of lawbreakers got off the hook, but I see you didn't learn your lesson. After you were rightly fired from your stagecoach job, it appears you joined up with this group of settlers, this California Congress, so you could carry on your nefarious activities here in Missouri."

Metz figured he may as well lie. "I was only driving a stagecoach, on my regular route. I didn't know I was carrying runaway slaves. A Mr. Smith told me they were his servants."

"Well," said the judge, "Mr. Smith is not here to corroborate your story. In fact, he was one of the ringleaders."

"This court sentences you to three years in the Missouri State Penitentiary at Jefferson City. I advise you to leave this state after you have done cooled your heels."

Metz was stunned. "But your honor, I didn't come here to steal slaves. I just hired on to escort these settlers to the West."

Judge McCall gestured towards some members of the California Congress.

"These good people assured me that they were intent on getting on out to California and that they were as afraid of you as they were of any bushwhacker they might meet. I've heard their testimony, that you forced yourself on them with threats and promises of money to be made by stealing slaves. They did, however, corroborate your version in the matter of Mr. Adams."

Judge McCall waved at the California Congress settlers while Metz glared at them. He knew they saved themselves at his expense.

"You people be on your way, and be careful who you associate with on your way West."

Looking at Metz, Judge McCall said, "Take him away."

Chapter 8

THE WALLS

Guards escorted Metz and three other new prisoners into the Missouri State Penitentiary across the Missouri River from Jefferson City. Once inside the prison guards pushed them into an open expanse flanked by cells going up three stories. The warden greeted them there.

"This area," and here the warden gestured with a sweeping motion, "is the yard, where you can stretch your legs from time to time. You will keep the yard clean; no debris, no roughhousing, no gathering more than two of you at a time."

The new prisoners kept their faces turned towards the ground in front of them.

"You criminals are here due to various offenses contrary to the law. You will serve your time until your sentence is completed. Infractions on our rules add to your sentence and may result in loss of privileges, such as being able to leave your cell and stroll about the yard."

"Now, some of you may be thinking that you will take your leave without completing your sentence. I warn you not to try. The yard is also where corporal punishment is delivered to certain offenders." The warden turned to one of the guards. "Bring out Copley."

Guards led the inmate Copley to two posts set about four feet apart at one end of the yard and tied a hand to each post. The inmate began to sob. "I won't try to escape again, sir, I promise."

"Oh," said the warden, "I hope not, for your sake." He motioned to a guard who ripped the shirt from Copley's back. The guard stepped back from the trembling man, who faced away from the warden and new prisoners. The warden commanded, "Proceed," and the guard uncoiled a whip, stepped forward and swung at Copley's back. Copley shrieked, his cries grew louder at first then died away to sobs.

"This is what happens when you try to escape the first time," said the warden.

Guards untied Copley's hands and he collapsed, then they dragged him away. The warden gestured towards Metz and his companions. "Take in the new prisoners."

Guards escorted Metz and the others through processing, where their clothes were taken and they were issued gray trousers, striped gray pullover long-sleeve rough wool shirts and underclothes and socks. They were allowed to keep their own shoes.

Several other inmates were serving time for slave stealing or attempted slave stealing, with terms ranging from two to three years. Metz's cellmate, Hector Moore, was one of them. Moore waited until the guard left after settling Metz in his cell and shook his fist at the departing figure.

"Calling us slave-stealers," grumbled Moore. "As if we were stealing property." Moore puffed his mustache out with scorn.

"Slaves are property," said Metz, "according to Missouri law. Like horses or wagons, and we have that pro-slaver

Buchanan as president who uses the Army to enforce that law."

"When I get out in a year or so," said Moore, "I plan to break that law. I'll head to Kansas and join the fight. We're little more than slaves in here, painting the prison walls or hired out to work for farmers across the river."

"At least you have a date to look forward to for your freedom," said Metz. "Slaves have no future to look forward to. I didn't have much of an opinion, one way or another about the slavery question, but now that I am looking at three years behind bars I can better imagine their plight."

"They have freedom to look forward to," said Moore, "if they can get away. I'm not ready to risk being whipped half to death for escaping."

"I've got three years before my day comes," said Metz. "I don't intend to wait that long. Unless things change I won't breathe air as a free man until September 1, 1863."

"You was just in the wrong place at the wrong time," said Moore, "but that won't help you get out of here."

"I'll have to get out on my own," said Metz, regarding his meal of mush and flour weevils with disgust. He tried to pick out the weevils but Moore stopped him.

"Hold on there," Moore said. "Them weevils is food. Just close your eyes, chew, and swallow. And don't complain about the food 'else you'll be put on bread and water—moldy bread and stinking water."

"I'll need my strength to get out," said Metz, "and I intend to get out somehow so I will eat the mush and the weevils."

"Oh," replied Moore, "getting out isn't that hard, it's staying out that's the tough nut to crack. There isn't much of a guard presence outside and sometimes you may be ordered to work for a farmer or other business in the town across the river. All you got to do is slip into the Missouri

River and swim a few hundred miles to Kansas; but, if you get caught you're going to wear red stripes on your back from the whipping you'll get. Or, they might go ahead and hang you. They do that sometimes, to second-time escapees, as an example for the rest of us."

Metz nodded but began studying the routines and eavesdropping on guards' conversations. The prison warden had decided some years ago that prisoners must be kept busy and he kept them painting the walls, inside and out, so much so that the Missouri Penitentiary at Jefferson City was called "The Walls." Metz painted, glad for the opportunity of some exercise, particularly when the warden had prisoners painting on the outside.

During his time in prison, Metz and other prisoners learned that several states had joined South Carolina, which seceded in December, 1860. Florida, Mississippi, Georgia, Alabama, and Louisiana seceded in January 1861 and Texas joined the secessionists in February. This encouraged guards to treat abolitionist prisoners more roughly than the other inmates, even those serving time for murder, and the warden made sure the prisoners were kept busy painting and doing whatever hard labor he could think of.

Chapter 9

ESCAPE

The spring of 1861 was very warm. By April Metz was ready to try for his freedom. A sudden assembly of inmates in the yard called by the warden in late April put those plans on hold.

"You abolitionist scum will be sad to learn that the southern states have had enough of the northern states telling them what to do. They took Ft. Sumter a few days ago."

The warden stood before them, grinning. Guards with clubs and guns stood ready to strike any prisoner who looked defiant. The prisoners fixed their eyes on the ground.

The warden continued. "You may know that six states have joined South Carolina and there will be more southern states to follow. Don't even think about trying to escape. Whipping will be the least of your worries if you're caught."

Metz did not respond to the taunting of the guards but gave up his plans for an April escape.

Finally, in May an opportunity for escape came, one that seemed tailor-made for Metz. The spring of 1861 was very warm and by April Metz was ready to try for his freedom although that opportunity did not arrive until May.

Metz studiously wielded his paintbrush while he listened to guards talk.

"Jeff City is getting culture at last," said one guard.

"What culture?"

"Why, the Great Western Players, that's who."

"What's so great about that bunch?"

"Toast of Europe and New York," said the guard, "according to the newspaper. They're heading out on their tour of the West. They'll be catching a riverboat to Westport once they get to Jeff City."

"So, what are they," asked the second guard, "some kind of burlesque?"

"Not at all. Sorry to disappoint you, but this is a high-toned bunch, doing bits from Shakespeare and what not."

"What kind of what not?"

"Oh, I forgot you can't read, or don't read. This bunch takes pieces from newspaper serials, like *Varney the Vampire, Great Expectations*, and I guess whatever they think audiences will like."

"No burlesque," said the second guard. "Guess I'll give them a miss."

"Don't matter no how. The Players will get here, play a couple of nights, and head off for Westport."

The night before his escape Moore held out a can of lard to Metz. "I got this from one of the boys assigned to help the cooks. You grease yourself down good and proper. That'll keep some of the Missouri River cold at bay. You don't want to cramp up and drown."

No one wanted to try his luck and break out with Metz, but no one would take the risk of betraying him either. Betrayers usually met a sudden, violent, and painful death. So it was the evening before the Great Western Players were to set out by riverboat to Westport that Metz's fellow inmates created a ruckus to cause confusion on the part of the guards.

Shouting loud enough for the guards to hear, Moore

yelled a question to a fellow inmate.

"Isn't Metz back with the paint yet?"

"He might have trouble finding it," said the inmate. "I told him to get some new brushes, too."

"I thought he was going to see the doc on account of his lumbago," said another.

"Excuse me, Captain," said Moore. "Can I go hurry up Metz? We ain't got that much light left."

"What you don't do today," said the guard, "you will do tomorrow. If Metz is goldbricking, so much the worse it will be for him."

While his fellow inmates were distracting the guard, Charles Metz stole away from the working party that was painting the outside walls of the penitentiary. There in the brush Metz stripped off his prison garb, greased down as advised by Moore, and re-donned his clothes. He found the dry log, thoughtfully placed in the brush by Moore, and slid into the Missouri River. The water was cold but the old Missouri wasn't running fast and the lure of freedom added energy to his efforts. He didn't try to swim upstream, but instead used the log to help him swim to the dock area, where riverboats delivered and picked up passengers and cargo.

Metz slipped into the warehouse, quietly ransacked cargo destined for the riverboats, and found a crate of clothes meant for dry goods stores farther west. He wiped the grease off as well as possible, then rummaged through contents until he found clothes that fit him fairly well and, luckily, a valise that he appropriated also. He stuffed a change of clothes into that. Thus equipped, Metz hid in a darkened corner of the warehouse and waited for the theatrical troupe to arrive the next morning.

Pandemonium and confusion attended the departure of the Great Western Players. That late morning, Metz watched the bags piling up on the dock as the theatre troupe and other passengers tried to sort out their belongings. Metz, carrying his valise and assuming a casual air he did not feel, stepped up to the confused mêlée.

"Here," he said grasping two theatre troupe bags, "I'll take these for you."

"Why, thank you, kind sir," said an attractive young woman whom Metz guessed must be the ingénue of the troupe. She led him to her stateroom.

"I'm afraid I can't tip you," she said, apologetically.

"No need for a tip, miss, my pleasure. But tell me, what is it like with the Great Western Players? Do you enjoy it?"

"Yes," she said, "travel, acting with a nice group of fellow performers except for the leading man who seems to like the bottle more than he does acting."

"I've acted some," Metz said, "in New York, even performed with the great Edwin Forrest."

"Ohh," she said, "*The Gladiator*. Of course I've heard of Edwin Forrest, and *The Gladiator*. We don't perform it, even though it's quite popular in Europe and New England. Mr. Blandon says we should avoid controversial subjects, and slave rebellion is controversial right now."

"Yes," said Metz, "I imagine so."

Metz wanted to ask the young woman's name but was afraid he would be asked for his name in return, and he hadn't thought of another name yet. He bid her goodbye and hastened to the dock to assist other players with their baggage.

Metz repeated the ploy several more times, in the confusion passing as a member of the theatre troupe to the dock workers and as a member of the dock workers to the theatre troupe. He noticed a valise that no one present had claimed.

"What about this one?" Metz asked.

"That would be Bartels," said a male voice behind him. A well-dressed man in his forties picked up the valise and hurled it from the riverboat onto the dock. "Drunk again. He's not coming with us. When he wakes up we'll be well away." The man gazed at the valise, shook his head, and turned to Metz.

"I'm Myles Blandon," he said, "Bartels's former employer and owner and manager of the Great Western Players. May I offer you a small gratuity for your assistance?"

"Thank you, sir," said Metz, realizing this is when he needed to change his name. "Kingman Moore, at your service, lately of the New York theatre." Metz liked the idea of using an alias adopted from his penitentiary friend.

"I understand, Mr. Blandon, that you may be seeking an experienced actor to join your troupe." Metz wasn't sure about this, but gambled on what he had heard from the young lady and from Mr. Blandon's remark about Bartels.

"Perhaps," said Blandon. "Follow me."

Blandon led the newly minted Moore to the riverboat's theatre stage area. He blew a cloud of blue smoke up towards the ceiling and regarded Moore.

"Do you know what this is?" asked Blandon as he held up a solid white cylinder about six inches long.

"Of course," said Moore, who remembered its use in the New York theaters. "That is quicklime, or calcium oxide, used for lighting the stage. For a small stage like this on the *Mirabelle* two or three placed along the front of the stage should do the trick." (The "limelight" as it was called became synonymous with the idea of fame or popularity in the theatre and later came to mean the center of attention in any venue.)

"Very good," said Blandon. "At least you have some familiarity with the theatre."

"Very familiar," replied Moore. "I have performed many times before the limelight."

"That may be," said Blandon. "What have you done?"

Moore regaled Blandon with a somewhat padded history of stage triumphs in Shakespeare and some of the better-known American plays.

"Allow me the opportunity to show you what I can do," asked Moore. "If you like what you see just permit me to accompany you on your tour. I ask only the barest minimum in wages, knowing I am an unknown entity to you."

"I'd like to have an actor who doesn't need to get drunk in order to have the courage to act," said Blandon, "as did my former leading man. I would rather not take on that burden along with managing the players."

"I find my courage by reading the exploits of Shakespeare's characters, not from a bottle."

"What I can pay depends upon the receipts," said Blandon, "but if you work out I can surely use a dependable man. We're going to do selections from Shakespeare, including Midsummer Night's Dream, Henry IV, the swordfight scene from Hamlet and then two acts in two nights from that newspaper serial, *Varney the Vampire*." We need to have a lot of action to keep the audience entertained."

Moore demonstrated his acting ability to Blandon's satisfaction and the undependable alcoholic leading man was left in Jefferson City. The six original Great Western Players, accompanied by Charles Metz alias Kingman Moore, boarded the riverboat *Mirabelle* for Westport.

Chapter 10

THE MIRABELLE

B landon's troupe had fared well on their tour heading west. He was able to pay double what the deck passengers did so that his actors had their own private rooms. The rooms were small, being just large enough to fit a bed and a small dresser but they were far better than having to camp on the decks with no privacy. The *Mirabelle* had thirty small cabins surrounding the dining room/saloon.

"I was able to get you a cabin in our area," Blandon said to Moore. "You will find that meals on board this riverboat rank with any cuisine you have had lately in some of the finer hotels where you might have stayed lately."

"I expect so," said Moore, thinking about meals of weevils and gruel he had endured in the penitentiary.

"We will dine together this first time," said Blandon as several people Moore recognized from the boarding chaos took their seats. Moore was surprised but nodded and put a smile on his face when Blandon said, "I am pleased to introduce a fellow thespian whom I met in New York several years ago—Mr. Kingman Moore." Moore was pleased to see that Blandon readily lied when he needed to, or wanted to.

The other players gave their greetings and smiled at the newcomer, each giving their name as they welcomed Moore to their group. Moore took care to remember their names, especially that of the young woman with whom he had spoken after assisting with her luggage. He assumed "Alcie" was some kind of nickname for Alice.

An older troupe member named Frederick Dawson commented on Blandon's mention of New York. "So," he said, "I guess you rubbed shoulders with some of the luminaries of the New York theatre."

Moore decided that a bit of modesty was called for. "I did rub shoulders with luminaries when I helped out on sets and when I was asked to stand in for an actor. You won't have seen my name announced on billboards."

Dawson followed up on his query. "So I suppose you had a chance to enjoy Desmond Gayler's plays *Taking the Chances* or his comedy, *Our Cousin From the Country?*"

Moore knew that Gayler's correct first name was Charles, not Desmond. Was Dawson testing him? Moore, as the young livery hand and stagecoach driver, Metz, had devoured newspapers from or about New York, so he readily corrected Dawson.

"Oh, Frederick," Moore replied. "You mean Charles Gayler, not Desmond. Anyway, I did get to enjoy both plays, even joined J.H. McVicker on stage once or twice when another actor fell ill or missed his connection to transportation." Moore realized he had missed several years of New York theatre during his time in Ohio. He would have to be careful answering questions about New York.

"What about Matilda?" asked Grace Young, who had married Dawson but kept her last name for the stage.

Moore had read about Matilda Heron, and knew that she had received several favorable reviews for her performances. She had also been described as quite a handful due to her temperamental nature off-stage.

"I loved watching her perform," said Moore. "I kept out of her way, otherwise. She is a strong personality."

Moore felt the conversation was heading into possibly dangerous waters for him. "But enough of New York," he said. "Tell me about yourselves, what you have done and what it is like to be a traveling company."

The troupe reacted like Moore thought they would. "Actors are the same, worldwide he thought." The company immediately began talking about successes and failures they had and sometimes broke into various routines and roles they had performed on the stage. They forgot about New York at least for the time being and Moore relaxed and encouraged them to tell their stories.

After the troupe had dined and was settled, Captain Daniel Blodgett, dressed in double-breasted coat with shiny brass buttons and his head covered by a short-billed cap, asked the Great Western Players if they would like a brief tour of the riverboat. Moore bent his knees slightly and stayed at the rear of the group, always looking for a place where he could be shielded from view. The Missouri penitentiary was not far enough away for Moore's liking.

"Welcome on board the *Mirabelle*," said the captain. "We are so fortunate to have you here. The other passengers will be delighted to be entertained as we make our way to Kansas City and Westport."

Captain Blodgett and the Great Western Players assembled on the Hurricane Deck, the uppermost full deck on the boat.

"This," he said, stamping his foot on the deck, "is the Hurricane Deck, so-named because a constant breeze blows across as we move up the Missouri. It's also called the Texas Deck because that," said the captain pointing to a narrow cabin set slightly back from the middle of the deck, "is the Texas, which houses the crew. And that," he said, gesturing to a boxlike cupola that sat on top of the Texas, "is the Pilot House, where Mr. Jamison, the pilot, or I, steer the boat and ensure our safe passage up the Missouri. No one but myself or a crew member is allowed in the Pilot House."

Two tall pipes rose at least 30 feet above the Hurricane Deck. Smoke and steam belched from their tops, which were ornately worked, looking something like crowns worn by royalty. A bell positioned at the forward edge of the Hurricane Deck clanged twice.

"That," explained the captain, "is the Roof Bell, and two dings on the bell alerts the engine room to be ready for instructions from the pilot. He speaks through a tube that carries his message to the engine room."

"Are we passengers allowed on the Hurricane Deck after our tour?" asked Mr. Blandon.

"Certainly," replied Captain Blodgett. "Just be careful, because if you fall overboard we most likely won't be able to reverse course and pick you up."

Blodgett pointed to the fluttering United States flag. "That is the Jack Staff, flying our new flag with 34 stars, the last star added representing Kansas, which came into the Union just this year, January 29, 1861." The captain paused and his face grew serious. "The slave state, free state issue is so controversial I suggest that you do not engage in any discussions, definitely not arguments, over the controversy."

"I assure you, captain," said Mr. Blandon, "that our company has no opinion on these matters, isn't that right, my friends?" The theatre company murmured their agreement with that policy, Moore lowering his head and nodding in assent.

"Now the deck where your cabins are, along with the dining area and the saloons," continued Captain Blodgett, "is called the Boiler Deck. Below the Boiler Deck, is the Main Deck, which houses the engine room and carries our cargo and the passengers who didn't pay for a cabin. You have the run of the boat, except the Pilot House and the Texas. Our crew does need its rest and its privacy. Enjoy your voyage on the *Mirabelle* and I look forward to seeing the Great Western Players in action."

"Mr. Moore," said Blandon after the tour, "Let's head to the bar and discuss our grand tour of the West."

"Why that's very nice of you, Mr. Blandon," said Moore. "Please call me Kingman. I will join you for a drink, and then I really should be memorizing my lines for our first show." Moore felt obligated to join his new boss but didn't want to prolong his presence among the other passengers, and he felt badly in need of a bath. Vestiges of lard clung to his skin beneath the clothes and Moore had noticed some fellow Players sniff and gaze at him sideways. Moore hoped that a bath and clean clothes and costumes and makeup he wore when performing would alter his appearance enough to avoid recognition as the escapee Charles Metz. Actually, very few passengers had any idea of what Charles Metz looked like, even if they had read of his escape in a newspaper.

"I like a man who likes his work," said Blandon, steering the taller man by his elbow to the bar. "And I like a man who is willing to socialize, also."

The Great Western Players generally kept to themselves, needing some time to set up the riverboat's stage. Because the actors were repeating performances enacted previously they only needed a brief rehearsal time, with Moore easily learning his lines and working with his fellow actors.

Moore initially wished he was traveling faster but realized he was probably safest on the riverboat, just another actor with the theatre company. He learned to relax as the world of Missouri slowly passed by on the riverboat's 170-mile journey to Westport and Kansas City. The paddle wheels of the *Mirabelle* churned slowly along and Moore found himself enjoying those times when he was not rehearsing or performing. He took in the splash of fish, the chirps of birds, and the smooth glide of a hawk or eagle, even the smell of the river. Moore only thought vaguely of what he would do when he reached Westport.

In the days that followed, Moore became a favorite with the acting company, regaling them with his stories of the New York stage that he had witnessed while a young man, sometimes inserting himself in place of the actors he saw perform. True to his word, Moore was a capable actor and the theatre was often fully booked.

"This will help for drinks," said Blandon as he handed a few bills to Moore. "Food comes with the passage. Anything you want laundered costs extra." Blandon tilted his head and appraised Moore. "And maybe you could buy Alcie a drink, too."

Moore started to protest but with a smile Blandon stopped him. "Don't think I haven't seen you looking at her. Of course, she gets many looks from many men, many different kinds of men."

"That is understandable," said Moore.

"Yes," said Blandon, "And I'm asking you to watch over her. We protect our own here in the Great Western Players and you look like a man who can handle himself, as well as any men who press their attentions towards Alcie too vigorously."

"You can count on me, sir," said Moore.

"I pay our actors something as we go along," said Blandon, "and I keep back a small portion of proceeds for each member of our company, a savings account for the troupe because I think they would spend whatever they get right away. I have explained this to the other players and they all agree, not always with great grace, but they know I am right."

Moore kept to his room or enjoyed the night air by himself, sometimes with fellow actors, seldom mingling with other passengers. One fellow actor with whom Moore especially liked acting was the ingénue Alcie, but he was fearful that attempting too close a relationship might provoke curiosity about him on her part. Her dark hair and dark eyes contrasted sharply with his memory of the fair-haired, blue-eyed Becky Stuart, whom he now regarded as somewhat shallow and certainly not loyal.

Another benefit of the slow pace of the *Mirabelle*, about five miles per hour with occasional stops to drop off or pick up passengers or cargo, was that as he got to know the other actors, he trolled through their stories for news of the day and how they felt about the trouble brewing between Missouri and the Kansas Territory. Moore wanted to identify and avoid fellow actors or passengers who exhibited pro-slavery sentiments. He did not mention his own reluctant part in the slave state versus free state conflict.

Chapter 11

MR. SMITH, AGAIN

The evening after the troupe's third performance Moore was standing alone at the rail, enjoying a cheroot, when a man behind him said in a voice Moore recognized.

"All the world's a stage. And one man in his time plays many parts." Moore turned and recognized Mr. Smith, lately of the abolitionist mob that freed the captured slave family and imprisoned Sheriff Martin in his own jail. Smith was dressed in his light gray suit when he and Moore first met—looking like a prosperous business man.

"Kingman Moore," said Metz, and held out his hand.

"Smith is still my name," said his former stagecoach companion. "Sorry about the mess you got into on my account. It appears, to paraphrase the Bard, that you have had many exits…and entrances."

"No hard feelings," said Moore. "I learned from that."

"Well," said Smith, drawing a roll of bills from his inside pocket, "consider this meager compensation. I waited to contact you because I wanted to make sure you were alone and that no one seemed to recognize you."

"Can't deny I can use the money right now," said Moore. "So, you must be doing well."

"Picking clean a few slave-owning planters who ride down lonely roads is chancy business, but it pays well if you live."

Over the several days riverboat journey, Moore alternated acting in Mr. Blandon's stage company with long conversations in the company of Mr. Smith. Moore told him about his betrayal at the hands of the California Congress.

"I don't know why they couldn't go ahead with their lie about traveling to California with me as their guide."

"I guess," said Smith, "that the California Congress folks felt they should sever their relationship with you. You were expendable in the great scheme of things, besides, you attracted the attention of the law."

"In their great scheme of things, you mean," said Moore. "I guided them to Missouri and defended them against those bandits but they faded when it came to fighting, for themselves or for me."

"I suggest you taste the climate of Kansas for awhile," said Smith, "until you scratch enough money together to go farther west. This climate is a bit hot for me too right now, so I may head out to California after I've plucked a few more feathers from slavers. There's a war coming and I'm too much of an independent sort to wear a uniform. I suspect you're much the same."

Kingman Moore puffed on his cheroot and nodded towards the din coming from the gambling salon. "I'm more against those slavery bushwhackers than the free staters, so if need be I'll take up your trade."

"If you want to throw in with the fighting free staters you could do worse than join up with Jennison or Montgomery."

"Who are Jennison and Montgomery?" asked Moore.

"Montgomery settled in Missouri," said Smith, "but moved to Kansas Territory when his free state sympathies antagonized Missouri slavers. Jennison leads a bunch of abolitionist raiders out of Mound City, Kansas."

Smith accosted a steward who was passing and, tipping him well, requested he bring two short whiskeys. Moore didn't normally associate with passengers outside the troupe, but was willing to make exception in the company of his benefactor. To Moore's question of how he might get in contact with Jennison, Smith explained.

"Find your way south of Westport to Mound City, Kansas Territory, about 80 miles if you can get there without getting shot by one side or the other. You'll know Jennison when you see him, decked out in a fur coat and tall fur hat. You might think he is got up like some comic character, but tread warily for he's a man-killer, sure enough."

Then, one voice hee-hawed through the clamor inside that made both men turn their heads.

"Me 'n Shaw made it hot for them abolitionists, got one of 'em sent to the penitentiary, 'cept he escaped." It was the whiny drawl of McCabe, the slave catcher.

"We've got to steer clear of McCabe and Shaw," said Smith. "Nothing would suit me better than to send both of them to Hell, but we are in the wrong place for that."

"Yes," said Moore, "I'm trying not to draw attention to myself. McCabe and Shaw have seen me several times before now and that may be enough for them to recognize me."

"Let's continue the conversation as we make our way along," said Smith, "but carefully. McCabe and Shaw might recognize me too."

Smith nodded towards Alcie, who had just come out on deck. "You should talk with some of your fellow actors and see what news they might have. That young lady is certainly attractive enough."

As Smith walked away Moore looked over at his fellow actor, who smoked a panatela. "Good evening Miss Alcie. Do I have that name right?"

"Alcyone, but I let people call me Alcie. It's too much trouble to explain."

"Alseeonee? What kind of name is that?"

"Oh, all right," said Alcie, spelling out her full name. "My father was captivated by the Greek myths so he named his two daughters after the Pleiades, which you may know as the Seven Sisters."

"Of course, that group of stars that looks like a tiny version of the Big Dipper."

"My father knew that we would go away sometime, either by marriage or by work. He told us that when he missed us he could look up at the Pleiades and know that the same stars were shining on all of us."

"So your true name is Alcyone. What is your last name?"

Alcie looked up at Moore. She was a bit taller than most women of that time. Still Moore towered over her. "What did Mr. Blandon tell you?"

"I didn't ask."

"He would have said 'Gibson'. What's your real last name, Mr. Moore... Mr. Kingman Moore?"

Moore couldn't move or speak. Without moving his head he looked left and right and placed his hand on his pocket revolver. He watched Alcie to see if she might be signaling someone behind him. Alcie only looked up into his eyes, smiling like a prankster. Moore slowly turned around, saw no one near and turned back to Alcie, who said,

"I heard about a Charles Metz, slave-stealer and killer, who escaped from the Missouri Penitentiary. He escaped right when our troupe landed at Jefferson City. You showed up unexpectedly but everyone assumed you were with the dock workers."

Moore nodded. "Why haven't you turned me in?"

"I don't like loathsome slavers or those dirty runaway slave catchers." Alcie took a breath and turned her gaze from Moore's face and scanned the surroundings. "And I need protection. There are mean and nasty trash on board and they've got their eyes on me."

"Fair deal," said Moore. "But please call me Kingman."

"Very well Mr. Kingman, er, Mr. Moore, er Kingman."

"Damn that Lincoln anyway." McCabe's voice cut through the night air. He stumbled up to the Hurricane Deck where Alcie and Moore were and headed for the boat's rail. He made it just in time to vomit over the side. Muttering and staggering McCabe cast a belligerent look around. His gaze stopped at Alcie. Moore moved back into the shadows out of sight.

"Well aren't you just the one to make me feel better." Holding out some bills McCabe said, "Here, let me know when you've worked this off."

He was too drunk to notice Moore standing on the far side of Alcie. Moore stepped around Alcie, surprising McCabe. Hoping the dark would hide his face sufficiently, Moore took another step towards McCabe and punched him in his left eye. Then while McCabe was reeling backwards Moore stooped, seized McCabe's leg, and heaved him over the side of the rail.

A splash, then someone on the main deck yelled, "Man overboard!"

The cry came from the deck below. Moore and Alcie heard voices, feet shuffling, and the sound of a life preserver hitting the water.

"Damn," said Moore. "He's going to be rescued."

The man who pulled McCabe from the water winced at smelling his breath. "Why he's drunk as a skunk. Must of hit his head when he went over, too. That eye will be black tomorrow."

Moore gripped Alcie above her elbow. "Worse luck. Best we get to our cabins. Maybe he won't remember what happened."

The next day, Moore kept to his cabin as much as possible while Alcie eavesdropped on conversations. She heard that some drunk fell off the boat and was rescued but also heard that the drunk claimed he had been pushed overboard. Passengers did not accept McCabe's account of what happened because several of them saw how drunk he was the night before. McCabe swore revenge.

"I'll get that son-of-a-bitch and then I'll settle with his girlfriend."

McCabe and Shaw roamed the boat together looking for the assailant. Unfortunately, for them, and for Moore and Alcie, they decided to check out the play, having been so offensive that no one wanted their company.

The *Mirabelle* expected to dock in a few days at Westport, meaning only two or three more performances. Moore convinced Blandon to do *Varney the Vampire*, for the last two performances, saying that passengers would enjoy the hokey thriller. Moore also knew that he would be able to hide his identity better behind the heavy makeup he wore as Varney, plus the cloak Varney used to hide his face. Perhaps McCabe would be too hung over or just not interested in attending. Neither of the two slave catchers attended previous performances.

Varney the Vampire had barely begun when McCabe and Shaw stomped into the theatre. Moore was ready to make his first appearance, his face painted white, his lips and eyes encircled with lampblack, and what was supposed to be red blood running down from the sides of his lips. Passengers packed the small theatre area, forcing the slave catchers to stand at the back.

Moore saw them enter and continued his performance. The voluminous costume concealed his pocket pistol. Even as he performed, Moore planned on what he would do should one of the slave catchers recognize him. Bluffing would be the first option. Second option would be to flee out the theatre wings. Last option would be to fight but only if Shaw or McCabe pulled their weapons.

Things took a different turn than either Moore or the slave catchers anticipated. Moore noticed McCabe who, staring hard with the one eye that wasn't swollen shut, said something to Shaw. Then both men pushed their way toward the stage.

"That's the varmint what threw me overboard," roared McCabe as he pointed at Moore.

Alcie stepped forward. "And you're the varmint who tried to assault me last night. Mr. Moore was only protecting me."

This statement from the comely Alcie stirred the mostly male crowd. Several of them stood up and began to move menacingly toward McCabe and Shaw. Neither man had a chance to draw pistols before the angry crowd pinioned their arms and wrestled them outside. The two men might have been hurled overboard but for Captain Blodgett.

"See here, stop this foolishness. We'll have no taking the law into your own hands. We'll settle this right here but we'll have a proper hearing."

The men's blood was up but Captain Blodgett prevailed. Under his guidance and the stern vigilance of some club-wielding steamboat men McCabe and Shaw were pressed against the wall. Blodgett and the crew and passengers heard testimony from Alcie, a reluctant Moore, and from McCabe. Shaw and McCabe had already alienated several passengers because of their raucous behavior since boarding the *Mirabelle*. Alcie's description of how McCabe accosted her infuriated some who began to move towards the men again. Captain Blodgett addressed two crewmen.

"You will take Mr. McCabe to the boiler room and put him in irons. Mr. Shaw, you will watch your step unless you want to wind up being shackled next to him."

Moore edged back from the front of the crowd. The potential problem of being recognized by McCabe was solved, at least temporarily. Then Shaw spoke up.

"Say, let me take another look at this so-called witness, this Mr. Kingman Moore."

All eyes turned to Moore and Shaw yelled, "That's him! That's the killer and slave-stealer, Metz. He busted out of the Missouri Penitentiary."

Now things really were stirred up. Conversation buzzed around the mob. Then Mr. Blandon stepped forward.

"Gentlemen, the distinguished actor, Mr. Moore, has traveled with this company for many months. He is an accomplished actor and a valuable member of this troupe." Blandon looked at Shaw. "And Mr. Moore is handy enough with his fists to protect a young lady from trash such as Mr. McCabe and Mr. Shaw."

Blandon's comments quelled the mob as far as Moore was concerned, but several men wanted instant justice for McCabe. "I say we get rid of these skunks," yelled one passenger. "Throw 'em both overboard." "Shoot down the varmint like the dog he is," said another. Others held up a rope with a hangman's noose already to slip over McCabe's neck.

"We'll have no lynching, no shooting, and no taking the law into your own hands," yelled Captain Blodgett. "I am captain and the law on this boat." Blodgett turned to his crewmen. "Club down the first ones that disobey my orders." At this, the mob stepped back and two of *Mirabelle*'s men took McCabe down below decks and shackled him in the boiler room. He would have a noisy and sweaty rest of the voyage.

Blandon had the theatre troupe crowd into his stateroom. "It would be best if we kept a low profile the rest of the trip. It's only three more nights anyway. Remember, we must look after our own, as Mr. Moore has done."

At this, Blandon looked sternly around the group. "We must appear to the public as what we are, merely a troupe of actors. Avoid talking about the slave question, free state versus slave state, and anything else that might be controversial."

Blandon dismissed the actors but bade Moore to stay. Blandon thanked him for defending Alcie.

"Thank you, Mr. Blandon," said Moore. "I wouldn't be able to prove I wasn't Metz."

"I don't hold with slavery," said Blandon. "I don't care where you came from, or how you got to us. I only know that you showed up right when we needed you and you were there when Alcie needed someone to defend her. You are welcome to continue with us if you wish. Lord knows you are a perfectly capable actor."

"I need to think about what might be the best option," said Moore. "On one hand, traveling with the troupe gives me a kind of anonymity. No one pays much attention to theatre people or expects them to be interested in politics. On the other hand, being linked with the troupe would make it easy for McCabe and Shaw to track me."

Moore and Alcie drew closer to one another, Moore appreciative of Alcie's silence on her knowledge of his real identity and Alcie grateful for Moore's protection. It was probably inevitable that the two would fall in love. As they later lay in one another's arms they spoke of future plans.

"Where are you going after we get to Westport?" asked Alcie. "And what do you want, that is, how do you see your future?"

"I intend to have a future like the future I thought I had in New York," said Moore. "My parents weren't wealthy but we lacked for nothing. We enjoyed the theatre, riding in the park on horseback or in our fancy buggy. People tipped their hats to my parents. I attended nice schools and we had well-to-do friends."

"I envy you for that," said Alcie. "What happened?"

"The Cholera Epidemic of 1849 took everything away, including friends who ceased to be friends when our money ran out. Then the cholera took my parents. I had to flee New York City, just one step ahead of my father's creditors."

"I'm sorry about your parents," said Alcie. "At least you had a good life for awhile. I'm still looking for that good life. After mother died, father took to drinking but quit when he realized he was in danger of losing his daughters. We understood and encouraged him to get help. He was able to support us with acting in the theatre and working on theatre sets. We weren't starving, but we never went for carriage rides in a park. I guess I caught the acting bug from my father. It is good to be able to slip into another character with a different history than my own."

"I mean to get back the kind of life I had in New York. I thought I was on my way to that as a stagecoach driver. I was even acting in the local theatre, moving up in society there in Ohio, but Fate had other ideas and cast me out of New York, then Ohio, then Missouri."

"Maybe you will find what you're looking for in Kansas," said Alcie.

"Yes," said Moore, "Maybe I'll drive a stagecoach in Kansas. It's a cinch I don't dare to do that in Missouri, even with a different name. Right now, Kansas is the only choice. I don't have the money to push farther west."

"But," said Alcie, "you don't seem to be bitter about what happened."

Moore smiled faintly and said, "It does no good to fret over bad luck. As Shakespeare noted in Henry VI, 'What fates impose, that men must needs abide; It boots not to resist both wind and tide.'"

"Pretty courageous words," said Alcie, "considering you are on the run, alone, and headed right into more conflict."

"I wouldn't feel alone," said Moore, "if I had someone willing to run with me." He took Alcie in his arms. "Would you be that one, Alcie?"

"Perhaps," said Alcie. "At least I know you will defend me but your life so far looks like it leads from one trouble to the next."

Moore said, "I heard that the state motto for Kansas is Ad Astra Per Aspera."

"To the stars through difficulty," said Alcie. "I know some Latin, being in the theatre."

"But it seems that," said Moore, "my self-motto should be 'Ad Aspera Per Aspera, "To difficulties through difficulties."

Alcie laughed and Moore joined in. Alcie rose and said, "Goodnight."

Moore murmured, "Good night," nodded and walked Alcie to her cabin, noticing her confident step keeping time to the rhythm of the boat.

"I want to talk more with you, Alcie," said Moore. "About our future, if we have a future."

"I've found a home with the Great Western Players,"

said Alcie. "A constantly moving home, but I will be with people I trust." Alcie grabbed Moore's jacket and pulled him close. "Come with us," she said. "Come with me. We can have a future together, even with the little money we will earn from the theatre." Alcie gripped his jacket more tightly and shook him. "If we part now I fear we may never see one another again."

"I'll find you," said Moore. "I will keep track of the Great Western Players."

"And how will I find you?" asked Alcie. "Will I look for Mr. Kingman Moore, or will you have another name?"

"Yes, I must have another name. My enemies, maybe some in addition to Shaw and McCabe, will be looking for me with your theatre troupe. My presence will only attract trouble for all of you. Neither Myles Blandon nor you nor any of the other Players should be in jeopardy because of me. I've got to go my own way for awhile."

Alcie wiped away tears.

"Besides," said Moore, "I won't be satisfied with the meager pay that I may earn as an actor. I don't look down upon actors or the theatre profession but I want to be somebody I can't be as an actor. Also, as much as I like Myles I want to be in charge of my life, not taking orders or direction from anyone. I have to make my own way, on my own terms. In order to protect you and the Great Western Players I must separate myself from you and the rest when we disembark at Westport."

"Ohh," sobbed Alcie, "I know you must pursue your destiny. Please stay alive so we can see one another again."

"I've been pretty good at staying alive so far," said Moore, "and with you in my future I have a reason to be more careful." He hugged Alcie, then gently pushed her away. "I'll find you somehow."

Moore began to turn away, then turned back and said, "And we can look at the Pleiades when we're apart and think about a time when we can be together looking at them."

Alcie nodded, closed her eyes, entered her cabin, and shut the door, leaned against it and cried as silently as she could. Moore raised his hand as if to knock on Alcie's door but lowered his hand and his head. He felt heavy in his heart, more so than when he got Becky Stuart's letter that dissolved their romance. He took a deep breath and walked away with no idea as to what he would do to gain the status and riches he sought.

Moore needed to think and took steps up to the Hurricane Deck. He and Alcie had talked late into the evening so passengers were in their cabins or bedded down on the main deck. Moore saw that he appeared to be alone on the deck.

Captain Blodgett didn't allow rowdiness or loud talking on any of the decks after dark. Not only was it disturbing to people just wanting to sleep, it could impair important information or orders to be communicated between captain and crew. What speaking there was, was done in low tones. A bottle's clink against a glass, the slap of fish jumping in the river, the glow of a cigarette or a pipe were all that broke the darkness and quiet of the night. The rhythmic drumming of the steam pistons pushing the big paddlewheel was more reassuring than irritating. The riverboat itself vibrated, lulling to sleep a crying baby along with the rest of the throng.

Moore leaned against the rail, feeling the breeze at his back and watching the big wheel endlessly turning. He looked back towards the Missouri Penitentiary, past Ohio, on to what he remembered of New York. "How did he get here?" he mused.

"Well, well," said a twangy, liquored-up voice, "looks like I got's me a fugitive. Dead or alive, too." Shaw cocked his pistol. "Now turn around, nice and slow. Hands up, Mr. Charles Metz."

"You've got the wrong man," said Moore. "My name is Kingman Moore, a member of the Great Western Players."

"And I," said the voice Moore recognized as Shaw, "am a member of the Church of England. Ah, ah, don't put down your arms. Only reason I don't kill you now is I don't want to lug your putrefying body back to Jefferson City, that and the pleasure it will be to see you put back in prison. I will shoot you in the leg if you make any funny moves. Hell, I might just shoot you in the leg anyway, just to see you suffer." Shaw, drunk but near enough not to miss, trained his pistol on Moore's leg.

"Of course if you attempt to do that," said a voice behind Shaw, "I will just shoot you dead. I doubt if there is any reward for you, dead or alive."

Shaw froze and turned, still keeping his weapon trained on Moore. "You!" he said, and saw that Smith had a derringer trained at his stomach. Moore quietly stepped to the side so that when Shaw turned to adjust his aim at him, Moore wasn't there. Shaw turned back to Smith who fired. His derringer cracked, not much louder than the snapping of a log in a fireplace. If anyone heard anything, no one came out of the Texas.

Moore caught Shaw as he pitched backward. Without a word spoken, Smith grabbed Shaw's legs while Moore held Shaw's body under his arms.

"Wait," said Smith. "We can't just pitch him overboard. Someone may hear the splash."

"Right," said Moore. "He already smells like he soaked in whiskey. Let's help him down the stairs to the main deck."

Moore and Smith shouldered Shaw up so it looked like two drinking buddies helping a third who had passed out. A passing crewman remarked, "Your friend smells like he's had enough for one night. Don't put him near any decent folk."

Smith replied, "We wouldn't think of doing that." The two friends got to the main deck and chose an area nearest the boiler, where its noise and heat drove away passengers. They carefully lowered Shaw into the current and watched as the figure floated a bit, was caught in a whirlpool, and sank.

"One body more or less," said Smith, "makes little difference along the Missouri River. We should check the Hurricane Deck for bloodstains, tomorrow, when we can see better."

No one on the *Mirabelle* missed Shaw unless it was McCabe, shackled in the engine room. Moore and Smith enjoyed the next few days of the voyage, glad to be permanently rid of one of the slave catchers. "McCabe is luckier than he knows," said Smith. "And if his luck holds out he won't see us again," said Moore.

After the *Mirabelle* docked, Blandon and Moore stood together by the rail on the Boiler Deck. There was no reason to hurry. Disembarking one hundred or so passengers and their goods took some time and Blandon used that waiting period to try and talk Moore into continuing with the Great Western Players. "Come on to California with us," urged Blandon. "Can't promise you much money but the chances of you getting shot will be a lot less in California than in Kansas."

"I think it would be best if I were to go my own way when we get to Westport," said Moore. "McCabe and Shaw know you are associated with me. I don't want to attract unwelcome attention to you. I'm in your debt."

"I haven't noticed Shaw around," said Blandon.

"Maybe he fell overboard," said Moore.

"If so," said Blandon, "good riddance."

Blandon peeled off some banknotes and handed them to Moore. "You earned this and more. If you want to find me or any of the other players, Miss Alcie for instance, just inquire about the Great Western Players. We'll be in this area for a while before moving on west."

Moore thanked him and Smith met Moore up on the Hurricane Deck, which was empty due to passengers clearing out of the boat and the Mirabelle crew busy with their work. Both men looked around the carefully, searching for bloodstains, but Smith's shot had hit Shaw in the heart, stopping blood flow.

Smith told Moore to meet him at a livery stable he knew of on the edge of town. "The Army usually gets the best horses," Smith said, "but the right price will fetch the right horse for each of us. Let me get there first and do a little bargaining, kind of get the lay of the land. After all, I am not a wanted fugitive."

Moore found his way to the livery stable recommended by Smith but as he began to enter the dimly lit stable he heard the nasal whine of McCabe, his voice raised in glee. "Ain't you a sight for sore eyes," chortled McCabe, "the leader of the Rescuers."

Moore edged into the shadows by the entrance and saw McCabe holding a pistol aimed at Smith's belly.

"Now don't be shy, Mr. Smith," said McCabe. "Let's just us take a little walk out back." McCabe prodded Smith in the belly with his pistol. "Turn around and walk real slow out the back."

Smith turned and began to walk as McCabe directed. Both men stopped their movement when they heard the click of Moore's revolver being cocked.

McCabe whirled around quickly but Moore's Colt boomed and blew McCabe back against Smith. The livery operator ran up clutching his pistol.

Smith said, "This fellow just tried to rob me. I think he meant to kill me too, but this stranger came by right in the nick of time."

The livery operator turned over McCabe's still figure, the dead man's hand still holding the pistol he meant to use on Smith.

"I know this bird," he said. "Nasty piece of work. I figured he was up to no good and I was just coming along to check on what he was up to. I think he was fixing to take one of my horses." He turned to Moore. "You the one what shot him?"

"Yes," said Moore. "I came along at the right time for this gentleman here, Mr...?"

"Smith's the name, and I am sure beholding to you, stranger," Smith said. He turned to the livery hand. "I don't suppose there is any question about who here deserved to be shot?"

"Not in my mind," said the livery hand. "Probably saved me from getting a horse stolen and maybe getting shot by that no-good, too."

Smith rolled out some bills and handed them to the livery hand. "No use you having to pay his funeral expenses. Also, I need a good horse and tack. It looks like my savior here does too." Smith peeled off some more greenbacks. "Here's payment for my rescuer's horse and tack, also. Little enough, considering he just saved my life."

The livery man left to notify the sheriff and undertaker saying. "I don't see a need to have the sheriff question you about what happened." He pointed to McCabe. "Good riddance." Turning back to the two, he added, "I've got a good horse for each of you." With that, he brought out two fine-looking mounts and pointed to the stable wall, where hung various tack. "Help yourselves. What you've paid covers whatever tack you need."

When they were alone, Smith said, "I may head west directly or I may poke around Kansas and the border for awhile. I'm used to playing a lone hand. Jennison's band is too big for me. You on the other hand would do well to get lost in a larger group. Also, it seems like you've worn out the Moore alias," said Smith.

"Yes," said Moore. "I need a new name and a fast horse. And I've got to find Jennison."

Chapter 12

JENNISON

Moore had a fast horse. He needed a new name. Thinking back to the state where all his troubles began he settled on the last name of Cleveland. He liked the idea of using the name of a city in the state that had evicted him. He needed a first name and had liked the first name of Kingman, because it implied high status. Of course, Kingman wouldn't do any longer. He wanted a first name that implied status and authority. Marshall had a nice ring to it, there also being the possibility that people who didn't know him might think he was a marshal, a lawman. "Marshall Cleveland," the former Moore said to himself. "That is who I will be for now."

The newly born Marshall Cleveland left Smith and Westport and made his way south to Mound City. The two Walker Colts he wore and his naturally imposing figure dissuaded the curious and potential troublemakers. As Cleveland rode south he avoided other travelers as much as possible. In this violent land people tended to avoid strangers unless they traveled together in groups.

It wasn't difficult to find Jennison's headquarters, nor was it difficult to identify Jennison among the mob of armed men at the Mound City Tavern. Before Moore could introduce himself, one of Jennison's men accosted him.

"Say," he said, "I ain't seen you before, stranger. Where you from?"

"My name is Cleveland, Marshall Cleveland. From Ohio via Missouri."

"You better not be no Missouri spy."

"Six dead men would tell you I am not a Missouri spy," said Cleveland, "if they could talk. They correctly guessed I am a free state man but were too slow with their pistols." Cleveland didn't see any harm in exaggerating his history.

"Okay then, but watch your step."

Jennison's bearskin coat made him look half-bear as the bulky coat filled out his thin frame. His high peaked fur cap brought his 5'6" height close to Cleveland's. Guessing that Jennison might be sensitive about his height Cleveland took care not to put his six foot plus body too close to the abolitionist leader.

The milling crowd gathered around Jennison, who stood on the bar of the Mound City tavern.

"We're going to Missouri. We've all had enough of the slavers and Border Ruffians coming over here and terrifying peaceful settlers."

Men cheered. Some waved pistols or big knives in the air as Jennison continued.

"I, Charles Jennison, commissioned by Governor Robinson as Lieutenant Colonel, say that we do not care about your past political opinions. No man will be persecuted because he differs from us, but now, neutrality is ended. If you are patriots, you must fight. If you are traitors, you will be punished. The time for fighting has come. Every man who feeds, harbors, protects, or in any way gives aid and comfort to the enemies of the Union will be held responsible for his treason, with his life and property."

Even before Jennison reached the Missouri border his little company of 13 men increased to several hundred, principally from Missouri, men who had with their families been driven out of Missouri.

A Missouri man, a German emigrant who along with many other Germans had tried to settle in Missouri, said, "They call us lop-eared foreigners and laughed while they looted our homes."

Such a force was impossible to conceal and when Jennison's raiders reached Butler, Missouri, just east of Trading Post, Kansas, they saw the bodies of three men hanging from trees on the entrance to the town.

"Francis Farmer, Glenn Joad, Benjamin Forrest," Jennison said. "Brave men. They volunteered to scout for us."

Burns and cuts on faces and exposed arms and legs and feet indicated the men had been tortured. A sign hung around the neck of the man in the middle. It read,

"This is how we do business."

Jennison spat. "Only reason they weren't scalped is those sons-of-bitches didn't have time."

Missouri men who had joined Jennison identified the homes of pro-slavers. The raiders looted the homes, took all the livestock, and set fire to what remained. Cleveland grabbed a whitewashed board and using charcoal scrawled, "This is how WE do business" and laid the board at the foot of the smoldering ruins. Thus, did Butler and its citizens, innocent or not, pro-slavery or not, pay for crimes perpetrated by the Border Ruffians.

Chapter 13

SPYING IN MISSOURI

The Jayhawkers returned to their Mound City headquarters laden with loot taken from Butler, intending to continue their raid in a few days. Cleveland pushed through the mass of men and, taking care to lower his height, slouched down at the bar next to Jennison.

"Sir, I wonder if it might be a good idea to reconnoiter the proposed battlegrounds before heading to Morristown."

Jennison looked over at Cleveland.

"Sure, but to be caught over there means certain death and probably torture before that. You saw what happened in Butler."

"I think I can get over there and back all right."

"Give it a try. If you get back in one piece and with some good information we all will be beholden."

"I'll contact you as soon as I return."

Cleveland left and returned to his room at the hotel to plan his self-appointed mission. A disguise would be necessary and Cleveland's experience in theatre made that a fairly easy task. He decided that portraying himself as an old man would be the best role. Cleveland had played the part of Polonius, Olivia's father and Hamlet's victim in Shakespeare's famous play. He would, however, have to modulate his speech so as to not make it too flowery. Cleveland decided to be a patent medicine salesman. That would allow some florid use of words, common in pursuers of that trade.

Cleveland assembled his materials and loaded one horse with them. He selected a powerful bay for his main mount in case he needed a quick get away. That would mean, however, that his disguise or some part of his scheme had not worked.

It took two days to get to Morristown, Missouri, finally coming into the known gathering place for Border Ruffians from the south and east. No longer attired in his customary dark suit and string tie, polished boots and Walker Colts, Cleveland led his second horse, now festooned with patent medicines and liquor. He carried one of his Colts concealed beneath a shabby coat.

Morristown was just waking up when an old man led a laden horse down a back street to the livery stable. Cleveland didn't walk or stand as tall as his six foot frame allowed. He had transformed his imposing figure into that of a frail old man.

Cleveland thought a good vantage point to look over the town would be the general store. After that a visit to the hotel's restaurant would allow him to see a bit more of the people.

Because Cleveland intended to count men and horses, the livery stable would be the place to go first. A visit there would tell Cleveland something about the number of riders and how well-mounted they were. Also that would allow Cleveland to acquire information without meeting many other people. Cleveland left his good horse at the livery stable. He led his older horse down what passed for a main street in Morristown.

Cleveland didn't have to wait long to draw attention.

"Lookee here, what we got? Some kind of herb doctor?"

"Got anything for stomach pains?"

"I've got piles, can't hardly sit my horse. What you got for me?"

The sudden interest almost convinced Cleveland that he might have done better financially by going into the patent medicine business rather than scouting for Jennison.

As Cleveland dispensed medicine and advice he noted that all the men were heavily armed, at least two pistols per man. This was usually a minimal armament for fighting men due to the time required to reload the .36 and .44 or .45 caliber cap-and-ball revolvers. Horses carried extra pistols and a rifle or shotgun. The men were jubilant. Even though it was morning a couple of them toasted one another on the capture of Ft. Sumter.

"Washington, D.C. is next," one man proclaimed. "And then we'll hang Lincoln."

Irregular sleep and food, whiskey, and frequent combat produced lean, hard men, grown callous to taking life and property. A harsh voice interrupted the chaotic buying and selling.

"Where are you from stranger?"

"Back East, Kentucky, before we got turned out. Yankee banker took our farm so I just burnt it to the ground 'stead of letting the bank have it. Turned loose or sold my stock 'cept Ribbon here. I read medicine for a while and plan to set up practice after I read up some more. Got to get books though."

"Can you fix a bullet wound?"

"Sure, not as good as a regular doctor but probably good enough to keep a feller alive until a real doc comes along."

"What is this thing here?" A man held up a belt that had magnets fixed onto it.

"Oh, that is the Liver Magnetizer. Good for biliousness."

"Humph." The man laid the magnetic belt back on Ribbon.

"You boys know where I might get a bite to eat?"

"Sure, just go up the street to Maggie's Den."

"Which I'll do directly you boys is through looking over my offerings."

Cleveland made enough money selling patent medicines and "miracle devices" like the Liver Magnetizer to pay for his meal at the hotel and pay for grain at the livery. All the while Cleveland counted the men and horses, remembering names that were spoken. If he stayed longer he might be around when whiskey appeared. Whiskey would loosen tongues but could also make men belligerent. It was better to be away rather than take that chance.

After finishing his meal, Cleveland led Ribbon to the livery for his feed and to pick up his other mount. The livery had good horses and Cleveland was tempted to lift one. That wouldn't do, though. Stealing horses would put the bushwhackers on their guard so Cleveland finished saddling the bay and led both horses out of the stable.

The livery man paused in his work as Cleveland prepared to set off. "Say, I'll take that bay off your hands. Old man like you got no use for a good horse."

"I'll tell that to my son and his friend Bloody Bill."

"All right, all right, forget it. No offense meant."

"I expect you can point me down the road to the nearest town."

"Sure. Holden's a good 20 miles or so down that road. I don't know which one of you has the best chance of making it—you or that nag you're leading."

The livery man pointed to a dirt road leading off to the north.

Cleveland paid for his horse's care and the feed for Ribbon and headed down the road. Once out of sight he transferred half of Ribbon's load to the good horse figuring to make better time and turned west, back towards Mound City.

Two days later Cleveland appeared before Jennison and reported on what he had learned. Jennison was pleased.

"You've done yeoman work here, Cleveland."

"Thank you, sir."

"Rest up a bit and be ready to join us hitting that nest of bushwhackers and a few other places we have in mind. Pick a half-dozen men to go with you and cut off any of those murdering scum who try to get away."

Chapter 14

MORRISTOWN

The next day, Jennison's men gathered in front of the saloon that had become their meeting place. Jennison stood on a hitching rail and waved the milling crowd to silence.

"We've all seen for several weeks past how Union men fleeing from persecution in Missouri, have come to Kansas for refuge, how we and other loyal folk have offered what little aid they could afford to these refugees from the cruel and ruthless tyrants who have held sway in southwestern Missouri. We're going back into Missouri and this time we'll hit Morristown."

Cries of "Here, here" and so forth interrupted Jennison's speech briefly before he continued. "And you, loyal citizens of Kansas, exposed to invasion from the guerilla parties of Missouri, and being unprotected by any organized force, have remained idle spectators of a tyranny and persecution that is a shame and a disgrace to any civilized people."

Cleveland wondered about the reference to "civilized people," since the heavily armed men would have frightened away civilized people coming from back East.

"Enough! Enough! Enough! Now we fight!"

The crowd mimicked Jennison by waving their weapons and repeating Jennison's words. Finally, Jennison waved the crowd to silence and said in lower tones,

"Mount up. Let us ride in defense of our homes and of liberty."

Cleveland swung into his saddle. He knew no one there but Jennison. He would be fighting alongside these men and wanted to be sure he could depend on those around him. As the group departed from Mound City, Cleveland lagged towards the rear so he could observe Jennison's followers. He nudged his mount close to some men who sat uncertainly on their horses.

"I'm Marshall Cleveland," he said. "I just joined up with Jennison after running into slave catchers in Ohio and Missouri. I take it you are farmers?"

"Were farmers, you mean," said one man. "Had a decent farm in Missouri but I made the mistake of talking too much or too loudly about my pro-Union sympathies." He removed his hat and gazed off towards Missouri. "Some pro slavery men or anti-Union men ordered me and my family to get out or be buried on my own farm."

"So," said Cleveland, "no offense, but it seems that you are more accustomed to walking behind your horses or mules rather than riding them."

"That's a fact," said the farmer, "but I can't just give up."

"He's right," said another man who rode his mount with some lack of skill. "If we do nothing, those scum will just come right across the border and order us off the land we have now."

"If we had any land," said a third man. "Some of us have to live in barns or share a little house with relatives or friends." He pointed east towards Missouri. "They won't rest until they've driven us out or killed us. I choose to fight."

"Here, here," came replies from several of his companions.

"Well," said Cleveland, "look to your weapons. Make sure they are clean and ready to use. You men are brave, but don't throw away your courage by being unprepared. By that I mean be prepared with your weapons and with your minds."

Cleveland was pleased to see that those men who had been acting nonchalant about the coming conflict grew more serious and they began to check their weapons. He knew that in a mounted fray these farmers would not be able to move their mounts fast enough and most likely had no experience firing weapons from horseback. Some horses, Cleveland knew, were apt to panic at gunshots and run every which way, maybe buck off their riders.

Cleveland noticed half a dozen men who looked like they handled their mounts with competence. He urged his horse to close with that group.

"So," Cleveland said, "It looks like you are experienced riders."

"Who wants to know?" said one of them.

"That's Cleveland," said another. "He's the one went in and scouted Morristown. Jennison thinks he is all right."

"If he's okay with Jennison," said another, "he's okay with me."

Cleveland engaged each man in conversation, asking him about his weapons and his experience with those weapons. Remembering Mr. Smith's admonition about personal information, he refrained from asking any of the men whether or not he had killed a man, or men.

"I see you're carrying one of Colt's Walker revolvers," he observed while riding next to one man. Do you have just the one or do you have another?" The man reached into a saddlebag on his left side and retrieved another Walker Colt.

"Very good," said Cleveland, and he went on to query each man who carried at least one revolver.

Close fighting would require repetitive firing and muskets, be they pistols or long guns, would be good for only one shot before having to be reloaded in the midst of a battle. Cleveland knew this would be virtually impossible, especially against their Missouri opponents. Those men often carried two more revolvers in saddlebags along with extra ammunition or already-loaded revolver cylinders with which they could quickly reload. The so-called "guerilla saddle" was designed to hold the extra revolvers and loaded cylinders.

Cleveland was no less articulate than Jennison, and though he was no orator, Cleveland could be persuasive. He selected six men who handled their horses well and who carried revolvers. One man in his group carried a shotgun in addition to his revolver, and Cleveland thought it would serve them well in the close quarters of the ambush he planned, so he chose him. Cleveland rejected a couple of other men who carried revolvers but obviously had not taken care of their weapons. He addressed the men he chose for his assignment.

"Jennison might have some special duties for me and I would be honored to have you men accompany me."

The seven men rode together at the rear of Jennison's force and when the party neared Morristown Jennison sent for Cleveland.

"Cleveland, take the men you have selected around the town and set yourselves up to intercept anyone trying to get away."

Cleveland returned to his group and directed them to make a wide path around Morristown. When they cleared the town and had a good view of the road leading out he had them line up just inside a clump of trees that bordered the road.

"You will do fine," he said. "Make every shot count. Pick your mark and shoot, and remember the homes you left in Missouri and the outrages you endured by the damned bushwhackers. You, Harper, with the shotgun. Empty both barrels at the leaders then get back in the trees and reload. Don't sit there like a duck on a log, waiting to be picked off."

"Shouldn't we wait on both sides and get them in a crossfire?" someone asked.

Cleveland replied, "No. I'm afraid we would shoot one another as well as the pro-slavers. And don't call out to them to surrender. Shoot them because they sure as hell will shoot you if you don't shoot them first. You two men farthest down the line shoot the leaders. You two men in the middle, shoot the next riders. I and these two men will shoot those at the end. We don't want to send all our lead at only one of those bastards. Don't hurry your shot. Make your first shot count because everything is likely to get confusing once the shooting starts."

The soft light that precedes dawn showed Cleveland that the men had positioned themselves all right—not too close together. He saw some men taking deep breaths. Cleveland remembered how Isaac, the husband and father of the runaway slaves described Gabriel as having a flaming sword.

"Easy, men. Remember your friends and family who've been beaten, robbed, and killed. You all have read the Bible (though Cleveland had little acquaintance with the Good Book). Gabriel carried a sword in his battle with evil. You will make do with your pistols."

He rode slowly back and forth behind his line of ambushers.

"When you shoot, your mount will most likely skitter around but that's alright. Keep shooting at the mess of riders. If you don't kill them they will kill you."

Pistol shots and the boom of shotguns shocked Cleveland's men into rigid attention. Cleveland shouted.

"They'll be comin' boys. Shoot them down like the rabid dogs they are."

Nearer-sounding shots. Hoofbeats. Shouting. Curses. Cleveland cocked his two Walker Colts and he heard the click of pistols cocking among his men.

Riding low, a dozen men burst onto the road leading out of town. When they drew even with Cleveland's band Harper's shotgun boomed. The rest opened up with their pistols.

The barrage lifted some of the fleeing men from their saddles. Some, wounded, held on and galloped away. Some fired back. Smoke from pistols of both sides hid the ambushers and those who fled. Five riderless horses danced about. One horse tugged at reins clenched in the lifeless hand of its rider.

Cleveland rode back up the line of his men. No one appeared to be hit.

"Good work. Reload," he said. "There may be more coming or maybe those sons-of-bitches will come back."

Cleveland felt drained as he reloaded. Some of his men slumped in the saddle, drained also. "Keep alert," he said. "The two of you up front watch the road. The rest of you keep an eye on this road coming out of town. Listen, and look for stragglers in the woods."

A few minutes later Jennison himself rode up to Cleveland. He surveyed the corpses littered on the ground and nodded his approval. He noted the lifeless figure still holding the reins of his horse. "Who shot that one?" he asked. "That would be me," said Cleveland. "I hope I didn't shoot an innocent man."

Jennison leaned over from his saddle and nodded. "Not hardly," he said. "That's Martin White. He murdered Frederick Brown, John Brown's second oldest son, in 1856. Justice finally caught up with him." Jennison spat a stream of tobacco onto White's shirt and turned his horse toward town, "We got some and you got some. Too bad we didn't get them all. Come along then."

Cleveland's band returned to Morristown and proceeded to complete the plundering. Jennison's band of two hundred Kansans and Missouri refugees came away with their spoils of war, valued around $2,000 in 1861 (about $60,000 in 2020). The victors took anything perceived to be of value, writing paper, hats, other clothing, horse tackle, bridle bit, soap, blank books, and an assortment of drugs and medicines. Some Morristown residents were neutral, maybe even silently pro-Union, but the raiders from Kansas seldom checked on the bona-fides of their victims.

Cleveland rode to the livery and took two fine horses. Jennison's attack had denied their owners the chance to flee, along with their lives.

Chapter 15

RIDING INTO LEAVENWORTH

R afferty kept his mount at a run until he reined to a halt in front of Ernest Renner's saloon in Atchison, where Cleveland made his headquarters. The dust was still settling when Rafferty dashed into the saloon.

"I just rode in from Leavenworth, Captain," said Rafferty, one of the six who had been with Cleveland at Morristown, "and they've got a wanted poster for you right there on Shawnee Street."

"Really?" said Cleveland. "What ingrates. This I have to see for myself."

"We'll ride along," said Rafferty.

"No, don't bother. I'll go by my own lonesome. I want to see if anyone wants to collect the reward."

Rafferty, Chandler, and House pleaded with him but Cleveland felt that Leavenworth had betrayed him.

"The Leavenworth crowd talked a lot about how they wanted to rid the county of Border Ruffians," said Cleveland, "but when it came to armed conflict they melted away."

A few hours later, Cleveland rode alone down Shawnee Street, in Leavenworth, and happened to see two soldiers walking along the wooden sidewalk.

"Hello there, boys," Cleveland called to them.

"Good afternoon, Mr. Cleveland," said one of the troopers.

"And whom do I have the honor of speaking with?" asked Cleveland.

"Private Simon Fox, Company C, Seventh Kansas Volunteer Cavalry, sir," said Pvt. Fox.

"Beautiful September day," said Cleveland. "Is it not?"

"It sure is, sir," said the second trooper, "and that is a beautiful horse you are riding."

"Well," said Cleveland, "It ought to be. Missouri has fine horses."

Cleveland had slowed his horse to keep pace with the two young men, but paused to read a freshly hung poster offering a handsome reward for the apprehension of one Marshall Cleveland, dead or alive.

"Tell me boys," said Cleveland, "do you think that's a fair likeness?"

"I don't think it does you justice, sir," said Pvt. Fox.

"No," said his companion, "That poster was not done by no artist."

Tall, handsome, erect and at ease in the saddle, Cleveland wore his customary dress of dark suit, trousers tucked into soft riding boots, a felt hat cocked over one eye.

"I just thought I should come into town and see if anyone wanted to collect the reward," said Cleveland, nodding to the poster.

"Not me," said Fox, eying the two bulges on either side of the rider's hips.

"Me neither," said his companion. "I believe we're on the same side."

"Wise choice," said Cleveland, and with a soft nudge he urged his horse to proceed down the street.

Neither the two young men nor did anyone on the streets of Leavenworth make any move to arrest him.

"Whew," Fox exhaled. "I think we were both close to meeting our Maker."

"From what I hear, and from what Cleveland himself has said, neither he nor anyone of his bunch has any quarrel with Union troops," said the second trooper.

"I sure didn't want to be the first," said Fox.

Upon returning to Fort Leavenworth, Pvt. Fox reported his encounter to his company commander, who in turn reported the episode to his commanding officer, with the news rising up the ladder of command, finally reaching to the office of the governor of the Kansas Territory, Charles Robinson.

Not many minutes passed before General Fremont, the fort commander, stood in front of Governor Robinson.

"What in thunder is the world coming to, general, when one of the most notorious Jayhawkers, this Cleveland fellow, rides right into town right past his own wanted poster and no one apprehends him?"

"Sir," began General Fremont, "Cleveland is one of Jennison's men and those are the men who are making those Missouri bushwhackers keep their heads down. We don't have enough men to protect the entire border."

"Well," said Robinson, "things are getting out of hand. Butler, burned and sacked, Morristown, burned and sacked, and most recently, Osceola, burned and sacked. There's going to be retaliation from Missouri."

"It's an endless circle," said the general. "Pro-slavery parties intimidate and abuse anti-slavery citizens, then the anti-slavery groups repay in kind. Don't forget that Lawrence was sacked and burned in '56, including destruction of newspaper offices and equipment."

Governor Robinson paced back and forth, lips pursed. "We're going to have troops sent into Kansas if we don't handle this. You know that will only give the Missouri bushwhackers the blessing they need to increase their attacks in Kansas."

General Fremont nodded.

"General," said the governor, "we've got to rein in these free-state partisans or arrest and jail them."

"We will do better getting them enlisted and fighting on our side, subject to Army regulations and discipline," said the general.

"All right," said Governor Robinson, "spread the word that every man who enlists will be given a clean slate. The men can elect their own officers same as other enlisted groups have done. Jennison and Montgomery have my authority to raise a volunteer cavalry regiment for service to the United States."

"Yes, sir," said General Fremont. "They will become part of the Seventh Kansas Volunteer Cavalry. I will see that word gets to Jennison and Montgomery that they must join us or fight us especially, Cleveland."

Cleveland was reconnoitering likely areas in Missouri, using his former acting trade, a master of disguise and guile. A few days after being visited by someone who passed himself off as a preacher, herb dealer, or whatever occupation fit the circumstances, that part of Missouri was visited by Cleveland and his men, who were charged with not always being careful to restrict their confiscation of goods to pro-slavery settlers. In response to these accusations, Cleveland sent a note that was published in 1861:

In response to these accusations, Cleveland sent a note that was published in 1861:

THE CONSERVATIVE, SEPT. 22, 1861

LEAVENWORTH

A Card from Lieut. Cleveland

I desire to state to the people
of Leavenworth, that all my acts
are done in daylight, and are published to the world. Property of
loyal men has never, nor ever will
be disturbed by me. If any person
will come forward and prove himself a True Union man, I will make
prompt and full restitution of any
loss he may have sustained at my
hands.

M. Cleveland

Chapter 16

ANOTHER GOODBYE

Before word got out that amnesty was possible, or because the word was deliberately not heard in late September, 1861, Cleveland and his men took advantage of the fine weather to proceed down to Kansas City. Cleveland, in the guise as a traveling seller of patent medicines, had met a man named Gilles, who was a slave-owner. He had praised the appearance of Gilles's stable man, who Cleveland referred to as "your hired man." Gilles had "harramphed" and commented that he was not bad for a lazy, uneducated slave.

"Maybe," said Gilles, "I will get more attention from him after I get rid of his lady and her brats."

"I've got some slaves I'd like to get rid of, too," said Cleveland. "Is there a local buyer you use?"

"Too risky to own slaves right on the border," said Gilles. "Damn Jayhawkers have no respect for a man's right to his own property. I'm selling them down the river."

"Right you are," said Cleveland. "I've got no use for help but if I can pick up some quick money I'd make a good deal for the buyer."

"The buyer's in Westport." He keeps his money at the Union Bank." Gilles sniggered, "The Union Bank, hah! As if the Union means anything."

"Very good," said Cleveland. "I'll see you next week."

A week later Cleveland road up to Gilles's farm outside Kansas City with a half-dozen of his men. He no longer wore the trappings of a patent medicine salesman.

"Where's your stock," said Gilles, referring to the slaves Cleveland was to bring.

"I'm taking your stock,' said Cleveland leveling his Colt at Gilles. They're going to Canada. You're going to Hell if you try to stop them."

Gilles said, "You've got no right to take a man's property. There's no law against owning slaves."

"There's laws that are right and laws that are wrong. Slavery's wrong."

"I'll have the law on you, the Army too," threatened Gilles.

"Your former slaves will need traveling money too." When Gilles hesitated Cleveland said, "The money will spend as well with bloodstains on it as not. Your choice.'

Gilles handed over a wad of bills. "Take it and be damned."

"And," Cleveland added, "I won't ask these people to walk to Canada. We're taking your wagons, too, and horses to pull them."

Cleveland had his men organize the fourteen slaves into three buckboards Gilles had as part of his freight business. He counted out several bills from the roll that Gilles had handed over.

"Here's some back wages for you," Cleveland said as he distributed some of Gilles's money to the newly freed slaves. "And wages for me and my men as well," Cleveland said as he pocketed the rest.

Turning to Gilles, Cleveland said, "Best you get on the road to California while you still can. If Jennison catches you he will hang you like the dog you are. If I see you again I will drag you before Jennison myself."

Cleveland assigned six of his men to guide the freed former slaves into Nebraska. "There's a Underground Railroad that'll see you through to Canada, or wherever you decide to go. We'll go with you as far as Westport, where I have some more business to do."

After the freed men and women departed from Westport with their guardians Cleveland, stood up in his stirrups and gestured towards Westport Avenue.

"While we are here, let's pay a visit to Mr. Harris, proprietor of the Harris House on Pennsylvania Street. He's a slaver and an anti-Union man."

Cleveland and his jayhawkers accosted Mr. Harris and took from him fifty dollars and two watches. Perhaps that is what occasioned Cleveland's arrest along with his lieutenant, Rafferty, by U.S. forces stationed at Kansas City.

Major Cloud officiated at the hearing for the two prisoners and immediately discharged Rafferty. Cleveland's hearing was postponed for the following day. In celebration, Cleveland visited Col. Ben Wheeler's Theatre, a venue that preceded vaudeville with fast-moving acts and bawdy comedy. As Cleveland entered, he was greeted by a crowded house rising, swinging their hats, and giving nine rousing cheers for "Cleveland the Jayhawker."

After the audience had settled down and Cleveland was seated a man approached him with a note. It said, "Backstage, Alcie."

Excusing himself from several admirers Cleveland slipped backstage and the note-carrying man guided him into a room. There he saw her.

"Mr. Cleveland," I presume," said Alcie, who rushed into his embrace. "I knew that Marshall Cleveland had to be you. My Charles."

"My Alcie," said Cleveland. "It is dangerous for you to be seen with me. I am still officially under arrest. There are too many eyes on me right now, and some parties would go after you if they knew we were together. I will send for you."

"I will get away after the show. I am still with the Great Western Players. We provide a better quality entertainment than the usual thing here, and Mr. Wheeler has us perform once a week."

Alcie slipped away after the shows and met Cleveland, who hoisted her upon his horse. One night together was all they had.

Charles dropped the nonchalant manner that he displayed to everyone but Alcie.

"Like an actor," he said, "my image is built on my façade, what others see, not what I feel inside. I can be honest with you, have to be honest with you. I don't know what the future holds, what Fate has in store for me, but I want whatever time I have to be spent with you."

"I am willing to run with you," said Alcie. "At least we will be running side-by-side."

"I may become legitimate soon," said Cleveland. Maybe I won't have to run anymore. Word has gone out that Jennison and his followers, me for instance, can enlist in the Army and I can raise my own company. Then I won't have to risk your life by seeing you. In the meantime, we have no choice but to part ways again."

"But not tonight," said Alcie, and buried her face in his chest. The night had passed too quickly, and the two had wrapped themselves in blankets warm from love-making. Light tinted the eastern sky in the pre-dawn haze.

Alcie looked up at Charles, "I want to memorize every line of your face, your eyes, your lips. Every time I close my eyes to sleep I want to see your face, remember the feel of your arms around me."

Charles wrapped his arms around her and pushed his face into her hair.

"And I want to remember the smell of your hair, the feel of your shoulders and the feel of your arms around me. We have to capture what we feel right now and keep that with us."

Alcie asked, "How can two people be so happy and so sad at the same time?"

"At least we have had this perfect night," said Charles. "Remember, you are never farther away from me than my heart. I will send for you."

Last embraces, last kisses, and the two departed with aching hearts.

The next day, Cleveland's sorrow at departing from Alcie was tempered by being discharged like Rafferty from charges of theft and horse-stealing. Apparently, taking money and horses and other plunder from proslavery men was looked upon as a duty, rather than a crime.

Chapter 17

CAPTAIN
MARSHALL CLEVELAND

O ffered the opportunity to join the Army rather than
be pursued by it, Montgomery and Jennison and
their followers enlisted en mass, becoming the Seventh
Regiment of the Volunteer Kansas Cavalry. They were
mustered into the United States Army on October 14,
1861. Jennison became colonel of the regiment. Cleveland's followers enlisted, becoming Company H, and
elected Cleveland as their captain. Cleveland, whose
followers had referred to him as "Captain Cleveland" before joining the Army was now a bona fide captain.

The next time Private Fox saw Cleveland, he was Captain Marshall Cleveland, commanding officer of Company
H, Seventh Kansas Volunteer Cavalry, so chosen by men
who had ridden with him as Jayhawkers. Such regiments
were often referred to as "the Seventh," "the Sixth," and so
on, without using the complete name of the regiment.

However Governor Robinson and generals Fremont
and Hunter felt about Cleveland, many people in Leavenworth appreciated Jennison and Cleveland and their
Jayhawkers in their efforts to keep the Missouri Border

Ruffians at bay. Ladies of Leavenworth chose Cleveland's Company H for the honor of receiving a flag they themselves had sewn and presented to him on October 17, 1861.

Two weeks later, with the regiment still at Leavenworth, the men marched out for dismounted dress parade. In Colonel Jennison's absence, Lieutenant Colonel Daniel Read Anthony, who had already made a name for himself in the regiment for irascibility, short temper, and a hectoring disposition, was to take the salute. The regiment having been formed in line, with the captains stationed in front of their companies, Anthony noticed that Captain Cleveland was in obviously improper garb. He wore his soft felt slouch hat and a regulation jacket over light drab trousers tucked into his boot tops.

"Captain Marshall Cleveland," the Lieutenant Colonel shouted, "what in heaven's name do you mean appearing in this formation out of uniform?"

"My tailor wasn't finished with my uniform," responded Cleveland. "I chose to muster with my men, rather than miss my appointed duty."

"Your duty is to appear in uniform," said Anthony, "not dressed like the freebooter you are."

"And you, Lieutenant," said Cleveland, purposely omitting the Colonel part of Anthony's rank, "are merely costumed as a soldier. Some men may respect the rank you wear but most see you for the popinjay you are, a costumed tyrant, fit only for a parade."

"I would call you a disgrace to your uniform," said Anthony, "but you aren't even in uniform. Return to your quarters forthwith and do not reappear until you have changed into the correct uniform."

Cleveland advanced from his position at the front of H Company and stepped in front of Lt. Col. Anthony, almost nose to nose.

"I'll beat thee, but I would infect my hands. Methink'st thou art a general offence and every man should beat thee."

At this remark from Cleveland, men in his company began to move towards the Lieutenant Colonel, but Cleveland waved them back. "Don't bother, boys," said Cleveland. "He's just a monkey in a uniform."

With that, Cleveland strode from the formation, mounted his horse and rode up to Lt. Col. Anthony. Cleveland maneuvered his horse so as to push Anthony away from the formation and to the front of the mustered men. Cleveland's right hand rested on the butt of his Colt and everyone expected him to shoot Anthony; but when the two men reached the front of the formation, Cleveland only turned his horse's head and brushed by Anthony, nearly knocking him down, and rode off.

On November 1, Cleveland submitted his formal resignation, which as a volunteer officer he had the right to do, and thereby severed his connection with the Seventh Kansas. Most of the men in Cleveland's company resigned also and joined Cleveland at his headquarters at Renner's Saloon, in Atchison.

Chapter 18

A CLOSE ESCAPE

Cleveland's participation with Jennison's band of Jay-hawkers and his own freelancing got him publicity that he had not asked for, but relished. As Smith had noted during their conversations on the *Mirabelle*, relieving slavers from their money and slaves was lucrative. Cleveland dressed in fine clothes and had a fine, expensive saddle, liberated along with the horse he took from a slave holder in Missouri. Men who rode with him called him Captain Cleveland.

Even though they were doing what some called "the Lord's work" for freeing slaves and their harassment of Missourians, Governor Robinson directed the Army at Leavenworth to give special attention to the area around Mound City. Cleveland realized he needed to move away from Jennison, who was attracting too much attention, and some of Jennison's band committed depredations that were attributed to Cleveland. He finally broke with Jennison over the issue of hanging rebels or suspected rebels.

"I don't hold with hanging men, as Jennison seems to relish, but we are all blamed for anything Jennison does. If I'm to be blamed for stealing horses and freeing slaves," he told his band, "I want the horses and the satisfaction

of freeing these people from their bondage. We'll move to Atchison."

"But isn't that too close to Fort Leavenworth?" asked Rafferty.

"It's also close to rich pickings in Missouri," said Cleveland, "And closer to the Nebraska border, where we can send our freed bondsmen farther north, safe from slave catchers. Look for me at Renner's Saloon in Atchison."

The Great Western Players had stayed on at Westport, finding that people there were grateful to be entertained by something other than the continuing news of border warfare. Late one evening while resting after a performance a hard knock on Mr. Blandon's apartment door roused him. Blandon opened the door to see a tough-looking desperado type standing before him.

"I have a message for Miss Alcie," he said. "It's from Kingman Moore. Is she still with the troupe?"

"I am a friend of Mr. Moore," replied Blandon. "Can you tell me what this is about?"

"I was told I could trust you," replied the messenger. "But I was told to deliver the message to Miss Alcie in person."

"Very well," said Blandon. "Please wait in my room while I fetch her." Blandon didn't want the stranger to know where Alcie was staying. A few minutes later, Alcie, accompanied by Blandon came to the apartment.

"Miss Alcie," said the stranger, "I understand I can trust Blandon here, so I am to tell you that your Mr. Kingman Moore now goes by the name of Marshall Cleveland."

"I knew it," exclaimed Blandon. "When I heard about the new border raider who had joined Jennison I thought that might be him."

"Captain Cleveland says that he is in Mound City, Miss Alcie, if you want to look him up. Or, you are welcome to join me now. I head back directly to Mound City. Captain

Cleveland asked that I accompany you if you wish to come. These are not days for an unaccompanied young woman to travel alone."

"Oh, Mr. Blandon," said Alcie, "I must go to him. I am dreadfully sorry to leave you without notice."

Blandon grimaced, but nodded. "Well, Alcie I hate to lose such a talented and attractive actress, and friend, but I understood the allure of heroes. After all, portraying heroes and villains is what the Great Western Players do."

The messenger and Blandon waited while Alcie put together a small traveling kit. Blandon hugged Alcie and grasped her hand in both of his.

"I wish you and Kingman Moore, or Charles Metz, or Marshall Cleveland, or whatever name he chooses next, good luck," he said. "You both will need it."

Alcie made her way to Mound City and found Cleveland shortly before he moved to change his base of operations. "I'm joining you," Alcie said to him, "on whatever journey you take."

"I can promise you adventure," Cleveland said to Alcie. "I don't know how much future together we will have. I don't see this conflict ending anytime soon, and I have both the Union troops and the Missouri bushwhackers after me."

"I'd rather be with you," said Alcie, "than only hearing snatches of news and not knowing if you are alive or even knowing where you are. And I am used to traveling, as you know."

"Mound City is getting too various with me at present. I've decided to move to Atchison," he said. "I will travel with you but only after you get out of Mound City. I think federal troops may be looking for me."

One of the former slaves freed by Cleveland, who had taken the name James Freeman, volunteered to drive the buggy that would transport Alcie to Atchison. Alcie watched as James heaved her two bags into the carriage. He took his place in the driver's seat and shook the reins to get the horse moving. He looked at the darkening sky and said,

"We're right on schedule, Miss Alcie. The Captain will meet us down the road. Time we get to the meeting place it will be dark."

"Thank you, James, you're so helpful."

"My wife and two children are on their way to Canada, thanks to Captain Cleveland. Least I can do is get you settled in Atchison before I head north to join my family."

Several miles farther down the road, a tall figure slipped out of the shadowy woods and quickly strode to the carriage. Alcie opened the carriage door.

"Oh, Charles, thank goodness. You know the troopers are looking for you."

"Yes," replied Cleveland. "We should move right along."

James rattled the reins and the carriage started off at a smart pace. The carriage horse was big and strong and the small group hurried through the night. Cleveland draped his arm around Alcie's shoulder. Both passengers relaxed and were close to dropping off to sleep when the carriage stopped.

Cleveland looked out the carriage window and saw a line of standing soldiers, rifles at the ready. Looking out the other window offered the same view. Lines of soldiers on both sides surrounded the carriage and two more men stood blocking the road.

"This is Captain Cummings of the Eighth Kansas. Come out immediately with no resistance or we will move on your works."

Cleveland turned to Alcie. "That means he is ready to order his men to start shooting if I don't appear. I'm going to get out and try to get away. I'll find you," he said. "Kiss me for luck and duck down in case there is shooting." Alcie kissed him and lowered herself to the carriage floor.

The soldiers relaxed as Cleveland exited the carriage, stood, and stretched as if he were awakening from a nap. They were close enough to touch him with their gun muzzles—too close. Cleveland rushed at the nearest soldiers, pushing them apart and into one another. The soldiers on the other side of the carriage didn't see what was happening. They were so confident of success they had grounded their weapons, even leaning on their rifle barrels.

Confusion reigned among the soldiers that Cleveland rushed through. He had knocked some down and they couldn't bring their rifles up as the Jayhawker dashed into the sheltering woods. He was lost in the shadows before everyone knew what happened.

The soldiers did capture Alcie and James, but there was no charge against them. They were allowed to drive off while the soldiers, especially Captain Cummings of the Eighth, fumed.

"You dunderheads let him get away. Don't just stand there, get on your mounts and go after him." But the soldiers were reluctant to pursue the Jayhawker, noted for his marksmanship, into the dark woods. They rode quickly into the woods but halted as soon as they were safely out of sight from Captain Cummings.

"No sign of him," said a sergeant. "No use stumbling along in the dark."

"And no use stumbling along into a bullet," said one of the troopers.

"Let's wait a bit before returning to Captain Cummings," said the sergeant. "We want him to think we gave it a good try."

Several minutes later the detachment exited the woods. The sergeant rode up to Captain Cummings and saluted.

"Not a chance to catch him in those woods. It's like trying to catch a black cat in a coal bin."

"All right," said Captain Cummings. "I know some troopers who are going to be put on extra duty after I break the news to the Colonel. He will be highly peeved that he wasted money paying off our informant."

The captain was right, and as the troopers paced their walking guard around the fort, they cursed the colonel and their captain as much as they cursed Cleveland.

The St. Joseph Journal writing about Cleveland's escape, advised, "The next party that attempts his capture had better shoot him first, and talk to him afterwards. By this means all can be made nice and comfortable."

Colonel Leyden held up that issue of the St. Joseph Journal and shook it in the face of Captain Cummings.

"The St. Joe paper has it right," said the colonel. "We just need to kill him and to hell with any talk of taking him prisoner."

"Shot while attempting to escape," said Captain Cummings, "if we ever get the chance."

Chapter 19

ATCHISON

Gentlemen," said Cleveland, joined by his former company, who had resigned from the Army also, "we are not going to sit idly by while those pro-slavers and anti-Unionists continue to wage their guerilla war against Kansas. We are going to carry the war to them and those who support them."

Bottles and glasses thumped on the tables and bar as his band expressed their sentiments agreeing with Cleveland.

Cleveland sat with his men around a table in Renner's Saloon. They had heard of his daring escape leaving Mound City and that news added to the confidence they had in their leader.

"While troops at Ft. Leavenworth sit on their heels lest they offend the secessionists," said Cleveland, "those very secessionists are riding into Kansas, knowing they can escape across the border and be free from Union troops."

"That ain't right," yelled one of his men.

"No," agreed Cleveland, "that isn't right. We are not hindered by military or political red tape, nor," and here Cleveland waved his hand east towards Missouri, "will we be hindered by borders."

"Here, here!" Men cheered and waved pistols, rifles, and knives.

"Prepare yourselves," advised Cleveland, "because soon we will take our revenge against those slaving scoundrels."

General Hunter summoned his second-in-command, Colonel Hardy and told him to get control of Cleveland. "I hear that Cleveland has declared himself 'Marshal of Kansas,' and is using Atchison as his springboard to wage his personal war against northwestern Missouri, absconding with horses mainly, but taking whatever else he covets."

"I'll see to it, sir," said Colonel Hardy. "I'll send a detachment up to Atchison."

"Don't worry, sir," said Captain Greeno of the Kansas Sixth in response to Colonel Hardy's directions. "My men will make short work of Cleveland and his gang. I'll send a squad of troopers to Atchison and bring him in."

Captain Greeno didn't see the necessity of leading the men himself and detailed a sergeant to lead them. The group pulled up their horses in front of Renner's Saloon but before anyone could dismount, Cleveland stepped through the saloon doors onto the boardwalk and drew his revolvers, cocking them as he did so.

"I will shoot the first man who draws his pistol. Keep your hands away from your side arms and dismount."

The dozen soldiers complied.

"Now," ordered Cleveland, "unbuckle your gunbelts and hang them on your saddle pommel."

The dozen soldiers did as directed.

"Now, gentlemen," said Cleveland, "get to walking back to Fort Leavenworth."

The men had no choice but to obey. A forlorn and footsore group of men ashamedly trudged back to their headquarters in Leavenworth. Several onlookers asked the soldiers why they were afoot.

"Did you sell your horses?" one wag asked.

"Looks like you sold your pistols, too," said another.

Cleveland, in the meantime, had several of his men take the horses with the soldiers' guns strapped to the saddles back to the fort. To the sentry, stunned by the appearance of a dozen cavalry mounts with no riders, Rafferty, Cleveland's right-hand man said, "It appears that some of your men lost their mounts and their weapons. Captain Cleveland returns them to you with his compliments."

Cleveland mused about his outlaw status, one he felt he did not deserve.

"Gentlemen," said Cleveland to the men gathered around him at Renner's Saloon, "We are doing the Army's work but not being paid." Men shrugged. What could they do about that? "So," continued Cleveland, "We will have to pay ourselves. Now, while our Union soldiers and our various militias are fighting off the slavers and Border Ruffians, banks in Kansas City are holding money the slaver villains get from their evil work. We will relieve one or two banks in Kansas City from the burden of guarding their cash."

A few days later, hoof beats of twenty horses broke the quiet November day in Kansas City. Cleveland and five men entered the Union Bank of Kansas City, leaving the remainder to guard against interference should anyone be foolish enough to try.

Cleveland strode up to the closest teller. "I must see the bank president right away." He hoisted a canvas bag up to the counter and slammed it down. "I am here about a substantial deposit. Take me to him."

The teller gestured to an office with a closed door and said, "Just a moment, sir," and knocked softly. "A gentleman here to see you, Mr. Dilman."

When Dilman came forward, Cleveland produced a pistol and leveled it at the president's stomach.

"I understand you support slavers by holding their money," said Cleveland. "Well, I'm going to be holding it now."

Dilman blanched and looked around. Cleveland's other men had their pistols drawn, covering the few customers. He unlocked the vault and handed over sacks of bills and some gold coins amounting to $3,000. The band next proceeded to the banking house of Northrup & Co. and took $850. (Author's note: The total amount of $3850 would be worth about $113,850 in the year 2020).

The day after Cleveland's visit to Kansas City, a citizens committee one half dozen strong traveled to Fort Leavenworth and there upbraided General Hunter. Adam Dilman, furious at the boldness of Cleveland's robbery, spoke for the group.

"Just when are you going to protect the citizens of Kansas City from these freebooters, General?"

"We have men out every day," replied the general. "We can't be everywhere at once."

"We've heard that story," said Dilman. "We've also heard what happened when your men had him in your clutches." Dilman spread out his arms.

"Your men came back, not only without Cleveland, but without their arms and their horses."

"We got those back…" began General Hunter.

"You didn't get them back," countered Dilman. "They were returned to you. By Cleveland. With his compliments."

General Hunter was steaming inside but he maintained an outward calm and, assuring the group that the brigands would be caught, had his visitors ushered out of the fort. Hunter sat alone at his desk, drumming his fingers on the desktop. He took several deep breaths and then yelled to his adjutant.

"Get Colonel Hardy in here. Now."

Colonel Hardy stood at attention before General Hunter.

"Oh, sit down, Hardy," said the general. "We've got to put our heads together and take care of this Cleveland fellow."

"He's got a lot of support from people around the state, even here in Leavenworth," said Hardy. "After all, he is freeing slaves, which is what the abolitionists want, and pro-Union settlers are happy to see the tables turned on those damned border raiders from Missouri."

"Truth to tell, Hardy," said General Hunter, "I'm glad we have someone like Cleveland taking the measure of them, and taking their horses, too. That at least delays them some until they can get fresh mounts. Trouble is, Governor Robinson is afraid that continued raids by Cleveland will give our pro-slavery opponents in Congress the excuse to lobby to send troops into Kansas."

"And that," added Colonel Hardy, "will hold down the Jayhawkers and give the Missouri raiders free rein to terrorize Kansans."

"And that," said General Hunter, "will lessen if not destroy Governor Robinson's standing with the free staters."

The general stood up from his desk and paced around his office.

"We've got to corral Cleveland, kill him if necessary," he said, "to show we're in control of the situation here."

Colonel Hardy stood. "I've got informers who told me Cleveland is planning another raid into Missouri. When I find out more details I will let you know and we will have troopers waiting for him."

General Hunter nodded and said, "Not everyone around here likes Cleveland. He's been named as the culprit in several robberies and horse thefts. Get some of those people together. We'll call them the Home Guard."

Several days later, Colonel Hardy met with General Hunter and told him that Cleveland and his band were planning to raid into Missouri and make off with slaves and horses.

"Gather the Home Guard and intercept them. Don't ask for surrender, just shoot them down."

The full moon shining through the trees drew black shadows in the snow. The moon's cold light showed shadows of seven mounted men, each man leading a horse. Four more men in groups of two pulled a sleigh in which huddled two families fleeing Missouri slavery. The warm breath of humans and horses crystalized in the frigid night raising a light fog that moved with the procession.

Cleveland held up his hand and the procession stopped. He whispered to Rafferty, "Tell everyone to take extra care to be quiet. We're approaching the river. It's solidly frozen so we shall have no trouble getting across."

Rafferty rode back down the line of men and the two sleighs putting his index finger to his lips. Everyone nodded, getting the message.

"We'll have the mounted party cross first, then help pull the sleighs up the bank. Don't start pulling the sleighs across until we've got settled on the other side. I will help guide our contrabands."

Across the river, other men waited for the procession to reveal itself. Two dozen pairs of eyes scanned the woods. Near-frozen fingers gripped weapons and men stamped their boots to maintain circulation in their feet.

Rafferty led his men across the ice while Cleveland and the four men pulling the two sleighs waited, just inside the woods. A slight mist, caused by the breathing of the ambushers, hung over the brush thickly growing on the river bank. "No reason for a fog this time of night," mused Rafferty. Then he heard foot stamping and rustling of movement as the ambushing party sought to warm themselves. He drew a pistol and slowly drew nearer to the bank. The click of many weapons being cocked caused Rafferty to turn his horse. He fired into the blackness and yelled, "Ambush, ambush. Get out, get out." Rafferty's mount was sure-footed on the ice, not so with the other men. Trying to turn too quickly they caused their mounts to loose footing on the ice and they went down.

Cleveland offered his extra horse and those of the sleigh-pullers to the escaping slaves, but only a couple of them accepted the offer. The rest were with their families and refused to leave them because they would most likely be returned to their owners. Cleveland told those runaways who remained in the sleighs to say they were forced to go with kidnappers who were going to sell them in Kansas. He then looked towards the river on which lay horses that had slipped and near the horses his men who had been dismounted or wounded. They were all holding up their hands in surrender. Cleveland rode away from the river into the woods, soon vanishing in the confusion of shadows and trees.

Rafferty, alone of those who were intercepted on the ice, managed to escape. He and Cleveland met at a spot already selected in the event of a catastrophe such as this. "We better lie low for a while," suggested Rafferty.

"Not likely," replied Cleveland. "I think I will go see that Marshal Holbert."

The next day, Charley Holbert, Atchison city marshal, was walking across the corner of Fourth and Commercial streets. As he raised his foot to step onto the boardwalk in front of John M. Crowell's store, hoof beats caused him to pause and turn around. Looking up he saw Cleveland, pistol in hand.

"Let's go for a walk, marshal," said Cleveland.

"What do you intend?" asked Holbert.

"Not to kill you unless I have to," said Cleveland. "Why did your men ambush us last night? I thought you were against slavery."

"Wasn't me or any men of mine," said Holbert. "I guess some people in town don't think the same way as you. Slavery is still the law in this country and stealing slaves, and horses, is illegal."

"Just the words I expect from the marshal of a town named after a Missouri slaver. You just walk along in front of me. I want to know what's become of my captured men and the poor wretches we tried to save."

"Your men were taken to Fort Leavenworth, where they will be given the option of enlisting in the Union Army or going to jail. I suspect they will choose enlistment. Those runaways are being returned to their owners. They said you intended to sell them once you got into Kansas."

Marshal Holbert gestured towards the next street over. "You best not tarry too long or you will be joining your men in Leavenworth. You can hear the Home Guard drilling now, can't you?"

Both men looked towards the sound of men shouting drill commands. Just as a column of men rounded the corner, Cleveland slashed Holbert across the head with his pistol, and rode out of town.

Chapter 20

A RIBALD STATEMENT

Colonel Hardy reluctantly strode into the office of General Hunter. The general looked up when he heard Hardy's footfall.

"Well," said the general, "what is it now? More Cleveland? I've heard about him riding into town and clubbing down Marshal Holbert. Too bad the militia was too slow to react to his presence."

"I think," said Colonel Hardy, "that they were in no hurry to confront Cleveland. All they had to do was march right around the corner of Forth Street. As it was, the militia, if you want to call them that, were content to make a lot of noise."

"That seems to be the case," said General Hunter. "So has Cleveland been up to more mischief?"

"Afraid so, sir," said the colonel. "He attempted to rob the Exchange Bank, right here in Leavenworth."

"So, you said attempted. Shot was he, I hope?"

"Only embarrassed, I'm afraid."

General Hunter sat back in his chair. "All right, tell me what happened."

"Well," said the colonel, "It seems that Mr. Alderson, co-owner of the bank with Mr. Hetherington, recognized

Cleveland when he entered the bank."

"And he didn't shoot him?" said the general.

"Sir, we can't expect a citizen of Mr. Alderson's position to be carrying a weapon, much less be able to use one against the likes of Cleveland."

"No, no, I suppose not, said General Hunter. "Go on, then."

"When Mr. Alderson recognized Cleveland he slammed the vault door closed and turned the combination."

"Mr. Alderson made a brave but foolish move," said the general. "Many a bank robber would have gunned him down as quickly as he shut the vault door."

"Yes, sir," said Colonel Hardy. "Cleveland isn't known as a cold-blooded killer. He did, however, make a ribald reference to the promptness of Mr. Alderson closing the vault, and went away."

"Hmm. What was this ribald reference?"

"Cleveland said that if Mr. Alderson was as careful keeping his wife's legs closed as he was keeping the vault closed he would not have so many different looking children."

Both men laughed, but General Hunter said, "I have to admit that Cleveland is as quick with his tongue as he is with lifting horses. Nevertheless, we can't have this robbing of banks, even failed attempts to rob a bank, happening in Leavenworth, where, by god, we have our fort! That damned Cleveland is making us the laughing stock of the border."

Colonel Hardy said, "I will send two detachments up to Atchison, early in the morning. Maybe catch him before he knows what happened."

"Good," said General Hunter, "and good luck to you. He's as slippery as a congressman."

Just at dawn, twenty troopers from the Sixth Kansas galloped into Atchison and reined in at Renner's Saloon. Only a few shopkeepers were out. The saloon was dark. Captain Williams and his men dismounted and rushed into the saloon. They only saw Ernest Renner himself, sipping coffee.

"Where is he?" demanded Captain Williams.

"Flown the coup," said Renner. "I don't know where. He and his band quit this place yesterday evening. They broke up into smaller groups and rode off in different directions. They didn't tell me where they were going, but they did pay their bill. I guess that means Cleveland doesn't intend to return."

When Colonel Hardy reported the latest news to General Hunter the general wasn't unpleased. "Maybe this means he is leaving the territory," said the general. "I don't care where he goes as long as it is away from Leavenworth."

Colonel Hardy said, "That fracas on the Missouri River cost Cleveland several of his men. I believe he has finally concluded that Atchison and Leavenworth are too hot for him."

Chapter 21

THE MISSOURI GUARD

Word spread that Cleveland had left his head-quarters in Atchison and several people believed that he had quit the territory. This emboldened some slave-owners who thought that was their chance to get out of Missouri with their slaves and other property.

A train of wagons with outriders left Westport in late March, heading for Colorado. The train included sixteen volunteer guards, armed with muskets to protect against Jayhawkers who would if not prevented, take the train's horses, goods, and property, including the slaves, which the train meant to remove from the reach of Cleveland and his band.

Caleb Brown, who styled himself as the wagon master of the little train, assured his fellow travelers that he would guide them along the California Road that lead straight west through Kansas. Brown tried to look the part. He carried a Sharps rifle and wore a bandolier of ammunition across his chest. His buckskin shirt had fringes that any frontiersman would envy. His slouch hat was canted over one eye, shading his round mustached face.

Brown waved the wagons and outriders onward across

the Missouri into Kansas. "Onward we go, heading west a bit, then to Texas. No slave-stealing miscreants got nerve enough to tackle the Missouri Guard."

"I hope you're right, Captain," said one of the company, Dr. Hardy, of Saint Joseph. He was a slaveholder who had refused to take the oath of allegiance to the Union and hoped to use his slaves to build a business in Texas. He cast a nervous eye at the surrounding timber, darkening as the sun set.

Brown thumped his chest and waved his rifle above his head.

"All you Missouri sharpshooters ready to deal death and destruction to Jayhawkers raise your rifles."

The sixteen-man guard waved their weapons and gave a loud "Huzzah!"

A voice from the shadows said, "Raise both hands while you're at it. Don't try to use your weapons if you want to live."

The men who had been cheering fell silent.

"This is Marshall Cleveland, along with some friends. Drop your weapons and dismount from your horses. You men in the wagons, get down from your perches. If I see a man holding a weapon I will kill him without another warning."

The Missouri Guard stood in a sullen group by the wagons and horses, their muskets and long knives scattered on the ground. Two of Cleveland's men herded them away from the dropped weapons and wagons.

"Do you mean to kill us?" asked Brown.

"Not unless you resist," said Cleveland. "Count yourselves lucky. If I were Jennison there would be sixteen slavers swinging from those tree limbs. I am not so bloodthirsty, but I am not a patient man. Move on down the road a piece, but don't stray."

One wagon held nine slaves and after conferring with them, Cleveland found that three of the former slaves could handle a wagon and horses. He instructed two of his men to ride alongside the wagon to make sure the newly freed slaves made the journey safely into Nebraska and onto routes of the Underground Railroad.

Before the refugees left for the North, Cleveland had his men look through the other wagon. They grabbed food, clothing, and farm equipment and loaded that harvest into the freedom-bound wagon. He selected other goods for himself and his band, then rode up to the chastened Missouri Guard.

"Empty your pockets. Any man caught holding back will be roughly handled. Just toss your money, watches, and everything else on the ground. So far, you haven't lost your lives."

The Missouri men, silent and apprehensive, stood in a rough circle around their former possessions. Cleveland handed a satchel to one of his followers.

"Now, you Missouri Guard villains, kindly fill Mr. Thompson's satchel. Rafferty and Gordon, look over those antique weapons and take any good ones and give them to our new friends, former bondsmen but now free men." Cleveland glared at the Missouri Guard and repeated while gesturing to the families he had rescued. "Free men, and free women!" Then Cleveland turned to his own men. "Jam the muzzles of the other weapons into the ground, good and hard. No, wait."

Cleveland turned to Brown.

"You, Captain Brown." Brown shambled over to where Cleveland sat on his horse. "You, Captain Brown, leader of this sterling outfit, get your men over to the weapons and jam the barrels into the earth, hard as you can. I better not see any man shirking."

Silently, the men grabbed the muskets and did as Cleveland ordered.

"Now," Cleveland said, "Throw them into this remaining wagon. We'll leave you two horses to pull the wagon, but you will have to take turns riding. It's a long walk back to Missouri. Just be thankful you are walking or riding on a wagon, alive and not swinging from a tree."

One man from the Missouri Guard took over the reins and six men piled into the wagon, sitting uncomfortably on top of the useless muskets. The wagon turned and headed back the way it had come.

"And," said Cleveland, "return the arms to Gen. Loan with my compliments. He's the Union brigadier general in the Federal Missouri State Militia. Tell him that the next time his Department sends arms into Kansas he should send them with men who can use them."

The shamefaced Missouri Guard delivered the arms to General Loan, musket barrels filled with mud, but otherwise undamaged. The men were footsore and embarrassed and some swore revenge. Others in the party quietly quit the Missouri Guard and sought other employment.

Colonel Hardy stood at attention before General Hunter. The general looked up, glared at the colonel and pounded his fist on the desk.

"Well," said the general, "I've heard about the Missouri Guard fiasco. General Loan, head of the Union troops there, is fit to be tied and is complaining to Governor Robinson. "If we don't do something about Cleveland I will be relieved of my command."

General Hunter placed both hands on his desk, stood, and leaned towards Colonel Hardy.

"And if I'm relieved, you will be relieved also."

"I'll see to it sir," said Colonel Hardy. "I'll get Captain

Greeno to handle this. He and his men of the Sixth Kansas have no love for Cleveland."

Chapter 22

CLEVELAND'S LAST RIDE

Alcie still called him Kingman instead of Charles sometimes, even Mr. Moore if she felt mischievous. The notoriety from Cleveland's liberation of slaves from the Missouri Guard caused increased and unwelcome attention from the Army but Cleveland believed they were safe in Osawatomie.

The days when Marshall Cleveland was Kingman Moore, or Charles Metz, were long gone but Alcie looked upon their days on the riverboat as some of the best ones they had together. When alone, the two of them would perform some of the theatre routines they had done on the *Mirabelle*.

"How long before you aren't Marshall Cleveland?" she asked. "That name is getting worn out, don't you think?"

"Men respect me as Marshall Cleveland," he said.

"All the same," said Alcie, "some of them want to kill you, and there is a reward for whoever brings you in—dead or alive."

Alcie hugged Cleveland and looked up into his eyes. "We should get out of Kansas, head to California like your friend Smith."

Cleveland paced around the living room. "You are right, of course. I need another name and another horse. I know that is what I should do, but it's hard to think about becoming a nobody again. People know and respect the name Marshall Cleveland." He gestured to saddlebags crammed with greenbacks and coins. "And it feels good to have money."

"Yes," agreed Alcie. "I understand you are proud of what you have done, and proud of the name you have made for yourself, but time is running out for you. It is time we get out of Kansas…together. I know I can't ride as fast or as well as you, but I'll find you and I want us to have some kind of peaceful life, eventually."

"We will, soon." Cleveland embraced Alcie and resumed pacing.

"Charles," Alcie pleaded, "they're getting closer all the time. One by one your old comrades are getting captured or killed."

"Yes," said Cleveland. "I heard that Rafferty got killed. Maybe I will have a way out very soon. A new friend, by the name of Walker, told me that he had a fine horse for me to look at. Maybe if I buy his horse I'll be ready to pull up stakes again."

Cleveland turned to Alcie. "You know, I am fed up with this life, too—not knowing whom to trust, knowing someone somewhere is plotting against me."

Unknown to Cleveland, his new friend, Walker, was plotting against him. Lieutenant Walker, of the Sixth Kansas Cavalry, and Lieutenant J.G. Harris, also of the Kansas Sixth, intended to have him killed by their troops, who had been embarrassed too often by the Jayhawker. Cleveland had frustrated every attempt to capture him, sending Sixth Cavalry troopers back to Fort Leavenworth on foot after taking their guns and horses or simply dashing away on horse or on foot.

They were still subject to taunts from citizens who asked them, "Do you know where your horses are?" or said, "Try to hang on to your pistols."

The two officers, under the command of Captain Greeno had no difficulty in obtaining volunteers for the execution they had planned. Walker's false friendship allowed him to identify the house where Cleveland and Alcie were staying. As Alcie and Cleveland were talking, Captain Greeno ordered Sixth Cavalry troops to Osawatomie, where they arrived at sunset. That night, Captain Greeno stationed well-manned pickets on all the roads leading out of Osawatomie and, at daybreak the next day, marched into town at the head of fifty men and surrounded the house where he knew that Cleveland was spending the night.

Sergeant Morris of the Sixth, was detailed to perform the first and most dangerous part of their plan—the arrest of Cleveland. He had ten men with him, hidden in the undergrowth by the house. When Cleveland answered a knock on the door he was surprised that instead of his friend, Walker, a uniformed sergeant of the Sixth Cavalry stood before him. Even though he had expected Walker to meet him Cleveland carried a revolver in each hand and had one strapped to his waist.

Morris said, "I've come to arrest you."

Cleveland said, "You're too short-waisted," meaning that Morris wasn't sufficiently armed, but that did not dissuade Morris, who had ten of his men nearby, and told Cleveland so.

"There are ten men right outside the door," said Morris.

"I can raise more than that at a moment's notice," said Cleveland.

"The ten men I mentioned are here now, ready to act on my command, and Captain Greeno has fifty men from the Sixth, sent here to keep you from getting away."

Cleveland glowered at Morris and lowered his pistol. "All right," said Cleveland, "but I don't trust going with enlisted men." Cleveland knew that he had embarrassed those men whom he had disarmed and taken their horses.

Morris beckoned one of his men to "Get the Lieutenant," and Walker strode forward. Surprised and chagrined to have been fooled, Cleveland agreed to go with Walker. "The joke's on me this time," said Cleveland.

The two men mounted, with Sgt. Morris and his men mounting to follow. When Cleveland saw the men had pistols drawn he knew this was not going to be an arrest, but an execution. He spurred his mount and broke away to urge his horse into a run south toward the bridge over the Marais des Cygnes River. A platoon of men emerged from the woods around him and opened fire. At least one bullet found its mark and Marshall Cleveland, alias Kingman Moore, alias Charles Metz died.

A reporter from The Southern Kansas Herald, Osawatomie, interviewed several soldiers, enlisted men and officers about the killing of Cleveland. He had a sheaf of notes from interviews of enlisted men who had taken part in killing Cleveland.

The reporter asked Lt. Walker to describe what happened. Walker responded, saying, "Cleveland agreed to go with me but as soon as he mounted his horse he drew a pistol on me and spurred his horse away."

"So," said the reporter, "Cleveland was arrested, yet you allowed him to keep his weapons?"

"Yes, I wasn't about to try and disarm him."

"Yet you had many men with you, one report saying you had two squads of eight men each and that Captain Greeno had fifty men sealing off the town to prevent his escape?"

Lt. Walker said, "It's one thing to have those men in the vicinity and another thing to have Cleveland right next to you."

"All right," said the reporter. "Let's go on with what happened."

"Well," when Cleveland began his attempt to escape my men charged after him in pursuit."

"And," said the reporter, referring to his notes, "I understand that Cleveland fired several shots at his pursuers and hit none of them. Is that correct?"

"Yes, that's right."

"But," continued the reporter, "Cleveland was known as an excellent horseman and a crack shot with revolvers."

"He panicked," said Lt. Walker, "He shot wildly."

"And yet," said the reporter, "Cleveland was known to be a cool head, and had escaped many times under similar circumstances."

Lt. Walker said, "Cleveland suddenly wheeled his horse and tried to escape, firing his revolver at the pursuing guards. His fire was returned, and he fell, struck behind the right shoulder by a bullet that pierced his heart and killed him instantly."

"Shot while attempting to escape, would you say?" asked the reporter.

"That's right," said Lt. Walker.

"We both know," said the reporter, "that 'shot while attempting to escape' is the classic mode of accounting for the death of an inconvenient prisoner."

Lt. Walker said nothing and the reporter continued, "One may doubt that any trooper of the valiant Sixth Kansas was a good enough marksman to score a bull's-eye from the back of a galloping horse; and in any case, if Cleveland was firing at his pursuers when he was shot, he would not have been shot behind his right shoulder."

"Doesn't matter where he was shot, or by whom, said Lt. Walker. Whatever the facts may have been, Cleveland is dead, at last."

The reporter turned to his notes again and said, "One account says Cleveland dismounted at the Marais des Cygnes River, emptied the revolver he had in hand and threw that and his watch into the river. This doesn't make sense. Why would Cleveland throw away his revolver, even though he had two more, and why would Cleveland take the time to throw his watch into the river?"

"You could ask Cleveland," said Lt. Walker, "if he were alive."

"And," said the reporter, "when I asked Sgt. Morris about the encounter he said that as the soldiers were closing in on him he fired shot after shot from the two remaining revolvers, but with such desperation and madness that none of them took effect. Really? No shots hitting anyone from someone known to be an excellent marksman?"

"If that is what Sgt. Morris said," replied Lt. Walker, "that is what happened."

"Another version of the event," said the reporter, "states that as he was raising his hand the last time to shoot, a private named Johnson fired a shot that pierced him with a Minie ball, which entered his person under the left shoulder, tore through his heart and nearly perforated his body. The account I heard from Sgt. Morris was that he was struck behind the right shoulder by a bullet that pierced his heart and killed him instantly."

"As I said before," replied Lt. Walker, "you'll have to ask Cleveland."

"I would like to ask Cleveland," said the reporter, "because there are conflicting stories about how he was killed.

A third version of the gun battle (here the reporter sarcastically said the words, "gun battle") is that Cleveland left his horse, ran to the creek bank and concealed himself under the roots of a tree. The soldiers searched the area, found Cleveland, and a soldier shot him with a pistol. The ball entered his neck and went down, piercing his heart and Cleveland died without a groan."

Lt. Walker remained silent.

"So, let's see," said the reporter. "In all this shooting, not a single man pursuing one of the best shots in the state was hit. Cleveland was shot under his right shoulder, under his left shoulder, and through the neck."

"Sufficient to do the job, don't you think?" replied Lt. Walker.

This time, the reporter remained silent.

Chapter 23

THE LAST WORD

B efore the reporter or the officer could speak again hoof beats and shouts interrupted the interview. A cry of "You bastards, you cowardly bastards!" caused reporter and officer to turn towards the shout. Alcie swung down from her mount and ran up to Lt. Walker. She shook off attempts by troopers to stop her.

"Where is he?" Alcie demanded. "Where is my Charles?"

"There's no Charles here," said the lieutenant, "only the Jayhawker Cleveland. He tried to escape and got shot."

"Got shot! Unlikely," replied Alcie, tears running down her face. "Where is he? Show me or by God I will shoot you, right here." With that, Alcie drew a pocket pistol from inside her jacket and leveled it at Lt. Walker. She cocked the pistol. "Take me to him."

Lt. Walker nodded assent. "Very well, miss," he said, and gestured for Alcie to follow him. Cleveland lay on his back. Alcie rushed to the still form and cradled his head in her arms. She closed her eyes, took a deep breath and gently lay his head down. Alcie stood up, took a step back and regarded her fallen lover.

"No bullet wounds in the front, I see," said Alcie.

"Shot while attempting to escape," said Lieutenant Walker.

"After he spared the lives of your men when they attempted to arrest him in Atchison," she said. "After he has refrained from taking any Union man's life while running circles around you." Alcie had held the pistol at her side and raised it, only to slip the weapon inside her jacket. Lt. Walker waived off troopers who began to move towards her.

"I'm sorry, ma'am," he said. "He gave us no choice."

"I can't kill you all," said Alcie, "and my Charles is gone anyway. I can't bring him back." Alcie looked down as tears ran down her cheeks. "I can't bring him back."

"We're going to bury him here, in Osawatomie," said Lt. Walker. "I will see to it that you are notified."

"I'm staying with him until you have done so," said Alcie. "My Charles, my Charles."

A little more than an hour later, Alcie watched as troopers from the Sixth Volunteer Kansas Cavalry lowered Marshall Cleveland, alias Kingman Moore, alias Charles Metz, into his grave. She stepped forward, grasped a handful of earth, and cast it onto the wood coffin. Two troopers finished filling the grave while Alcie watched. A Chaplin from the Sixth Cavalry read the official service for "A brother soldier whom we lay to rest. May he rest in peace."

Alcie stepped forward and said, "Earth counts one mortal less-Heaven one angel more."

"He was brave," said Lt. Walker. "I'll give him that."

"I will be back," said Alcie, "to see that he has a proper memorial." She strode to her horse, mounted and stilled the horse while she looked one at a time into the faces of the troopers standing by Cleveland's grave.

Alcie did come back, several months later, in August, to see that her memorial to Captain Marshall Cleveland was properly set at the head of his last resting place.

Sacred to the memory of

Captain Marshall L. Cleveland,

Who died May 11th, 1862

Aged 30 yrs.

Earth counts one mortal less-

Heaven one angel more.

Author's Notes

WHY CLEVELAND?

IT WAS WHILE I was researching the archives at the Kansas Historical Society that I ran across an incident account of Marshall Cleveland, written by by Simeon M. Fox, "The Early History of the Seventh Kansas Cavalry," Collections of the Kansas State Historical Society, 1909-1910, XI, 244-45. This incident was also described in Jennison's Jayhawkers: A Civil War Regiment and Its Commander, by Stephen Z. Starr.

CAPTAIN MARSHALL CLEVELAND

Simeon Fox, a native of Tompkins County, New York, and a graduate of Genessee College, emigrated to Kansas in the summer of 1861. On a September day, shortly after he had enlisted as a trooper in Company C, Seventh Kansas Volunteer Cavalry, he went for a leisurely stroll in company with a fellow recruit to view the sights of Leavenworth, where their regiment was then in the process of formation. The two young men had just paused on Shawnee Street to read a freshly hung poster offering a handsome reward for the apprehension of one Marshall Cleveland, dead or alive, when they saw a striking figure riding toward them. The horseman, tall, handsome, erect, and wonderfully at ease in the saddle, was a figure to arrest the eye. Thin visage, his complexion was sallow and olive-tinted, eyes black and piercing, hair and beard dark and neatly trimmed. He was dressed with conspicuous elegance in a drab suit, trousers tucked into soft riding boots of a glossy polish, a felt hat cocked gracefully over one eye. As he passed the two sight-seers, he revealed on either side of the skirts of his well-brushed frock coat the bulges that made it evident that, in the fashion of the day, he was equipped with the means of defense and attack. The horse he rode was a splendid animal, obviously a thoroughbred. As the two young men turned to resume their walk, Fox remarked to his companion, "That's a mighty fine horse," and the other replied, "It ought to be; he has the pick of Missouri. That's Marshall Cleveland."

If Cleveland was aware of the "Wanted—Dead or Alive" poster, it did not appear to ruffle his composure; nor clearly enough, did anyone on the streets of the bustling Missouri River town he graced with his presence make any move to arrest him....The citizens of Leavenworth were content to stand aside while Cleveland and the law settled their differences, whatever they may have been.

PURSUIT OF CLEVELAND'S STORY

Intrigued by someone who would ride alone into Leavenworth, right by his own Wanted—Dead or Alive poster, I decided to inquire further and searched through Kansas and Missouri newspapers publishing 1860 through 1862. Hours of searching might produce a single paragraph, or nothing at all.

SEARCH FOR CLEVELAND'S TOMBSTONE

Another feature of what I came to regard as the Cleveland legend was John J. Ingalls's, "The Last of the Jayhawkers," *Kansas Magazine*, I, (1872), 360. Cf. Fox, "Story," 23. Ingalls wrote, His "temporary wife" took him to St. Joseph and buried him, erecting to his memory the tombstone made famous by the caustic genius of John Ingalls. (Ingalls claimed that the tombstone carried an inscription, "One hero less on earth, one angel more in heaven" and on the reverse side was carved the figure of an angel holding a revolver in each hand.)

I wanted to find that tombstone and convinced several family members to go with me to St. Joseph, Missouri in order to find and photograph it. The cemetery records were destroyed in the 1951 flood and therefore we asked where the oldest cemeteries were and scoured their grounds with no success. I did find one interesting tombstone, however, which memorialized a participant in the American Revolution. I do not recall that veteran's name, other than he was listed as a sergeant. He traveled halfway across the continent to make Missouri his home.

Some years later, further research indicated that Marshall Cleveland was buried in Osawatomie, where he had been killed. I did find that tombstone although there was not an angel holding a revolver in either hand. It is possible that an engraved image could have been obliterated by 160 years of weather. The tombstone did say "One Hero Less on Earth, One Angel More in Heaven." I photographed that tombstone along with that tribute ordered inscribed by his mistress/wife. When I visited the cemetery several years later I found that the tombstone had been knocked down and cemented into the ground. I have searched among my photo archives and not found that picture.

Just recently I discovered the reason for John Ingalls's error. Kansas State Senator John James Ingalls wrote in an article published in 1902, that "His temporary widow took his sacred clay to St. Joseph, where its place of interment is marked by a marble headstone bearing the usual memoranda, and concluding with the following:

"One hero less on earth,
One angel more in heaven!"

Ingalls and others however, were mistaken. The authentic story of Cleveland's interment and of his widow was written in 1904, by a former wagon master and occasional express rider named R.M. Peck. Peck and his associate Dan Eckerberger stopped at a hotel in Osawatomie in August, 1862. Ushered into the men's parlor to await their meal, Peck eyed a freshly chiseled tombstone propped up in the corner of the room. Curious to determine the inscription carved into the slab, Peck walked over and read:

Sacred to the memory of

Captain Marshall L. Cleveland,

Who died May 11th, 1862

Aged 30 yrs.

Earth counts one mortal less–

Heaven one angel more.

Peck says he blurted out impulsively: "Hell's full of such angels," and saw a black-eyed woman 'looking daggers' at me, and I feared I had hurt her feelings, whoever she was. The landlord requested: "Mister, please don't use such language in the hearing of the lady in the next room. She's Capt. Cleveland's widow." The landlord informed me that 'Mrs. Cleveland' had recently brought the tombstone from Leavenworth to have it placed at the jayhawker's grave.

WHY THREE NAMES?

Newspapers' comments on Cleveland's death said, "The Jayhawker Cleveland, alias Moore, alias Metz..." My story describes what I believe are logical reasons for the different names.

WHY NEW YORK CITY?

Cleveland was thirty-years-old at the time of his death. Ingall's and other newspapers' comments on the death of Cleveland said that he had come from New York City. Investigation of events in New York revealed that was the time of the first 1832 Cholera Epidemic, so I was justified in setting his birth at that year and his name as Charles Metz.

OHIO STAGE COACH DRIVER

Additional comments from newspapers said, "For a time he drove a stagecoach in Ohio." The Cholera Epidemic of 1849 provided a reason for young Metz, aged 17, to be orphaned by the plague and fleeing New York to avoid his deceased father's creditors. Like thousands of other easterners he went West. In the 1850s stagecoaches were a primary means of travel and stagecoach drivers were paid well. Driving a stage took skill and courage, for Ohio had its share of highway robbers and a six-horse team required skill and strength to manage.

MISSOURI PENITENTIARY

"He had his first major brush with the law in Missouri and was sentenced to imprisonment in the state penitentiary."

Ohio, like many states along the North/South Mason-Dixon Line, had towns and counties that were pro-slavery and towns that favored the abolitionist cause (See The Town That Started the Civil War, by Nat Brandt.) That book inspired me to develop the reason for Charles Metz to lose his stagecoach driving job in Ohio and leave that state, acting as a wagon master, heading west with Ohio abolitionists who intended to make Kansas into a free state.

ESCAPE

My research into the Missouri State Penitentiary at Jefferson City showed that escapes from that penitentiary were not rare, though returned escapees were sometimes hanged. That prison has been variously described as "the Missouri Penitentiary," the "Penitentiary at Jefferson City," and even the "Jefferson City Penitentiary."

THE MIRABELLE

A riverboat seemed to be the best way for a fugitive like Metz, alias Moore, to get out of Missouri. Other newspaper accounts of his ability to pose in various disguises made it natural that he joined a traveling theatre troupe under the name of Moore. Also, I wrote Cleveland's story as one of the short stories I submitted for a short story writing class, English 551, taught by Prof. Thomas Lorenz. Everyone was intrigued by the riverboat sequence and wanted more action to take place on the riverboat. I researched riverboats in order to give readers a picture of riverboat passage during that time and to place other events there in telling the story. I really appreciated the suggestions by my fellow students and by Prof. Lorenz in developing the story.

KANSAS

THE DAILY CONSERVATIVE,

Leavenworth, Kansas, May 14, 1862

Then he drifted west. Having assumed the name of Moore he crossed the border to Kansas in the spring of 1861 and, perhaps as an echo of his life in Ohio, assumed the name of Cleveland. We believe the first appearance of Cleveland in Kansas was in May last (1861). No one seemed to know where he came from although there has always been a rumor that he was a convict who had made his escape from the Jefferson City Penitentiary.

THE JAYHAWKER

"Marshall Cleveland became popular as a fighting man at the time when Union men were so heartlessly driven from their homes in the border counties of Missouri and Kansas." Almost one hundred-sixty years after the events in this story one may easily get into arguments of Jayhawkers versus Missouri Border Ruffians. Both sides had rationales for what they did—right and wrong.

MARSHALL CLEVELAND:
COLD-BLOODED KILLER OR NOT?

During the Border War era and well into the 20th Century most towns had at least one newspaper and every newspaper had an opinion, sometime diametrically opposed to newspapers in its own or in another town. In my hours of research, although some newspapers called Cleveland a murderer I never found a reference to cold-blooded killing done by Cleveland. On the other hand, I found references to Cleveland disarming adversaries and sending them on their way without their weapons and often without their horses, so reported in The Morning Herald, 26 March, 1862, below.

SENT THEM BACK—There is a story on the streets that, several of our citizens borrowed some muskets—about 16—and started across the plains to guard a train of goods, etc. en route for the Peak. This was kind. This was patriotic. But the train goes Westward, and the story goes thus: Cleveland came up with the party, cleaned them out completely, and Cleveland, the jayhawker par excellence, very kindly told them to return the arms to Gen. Loan, with his compliments, advising that the next time the Department sent arms into Kansas they send with them men who could use them. Of course we do not believe the story. We do know, however, that the arms came back, safe and sound.

CLEVELAND ATTRIBUTES

OLATHE MIRROR

From the Leavenworth Conservative

His band has never been large, and he often traveled alone. His skill in disguising his appearance and voice were so great that even to those who knew him he seemed each day a different man although he was taller than six feet in height, and had a form as straight as an arrow. Some persons, blessed with more imagination than brains, believe he led a charmed life. They called him the "Phantom Horseman of the Prairie" and told strange stories of his prowess and good fortune.

During all these months he has led a wild, strange life. Soldiers have been constantly looking for him, and twice nearly captured him, but audacity, bravado and a cat-like stealth have been his preservers until now. (His death at the hands of the Sixth Kansas.)

It is probably true that this war, which, to a people accustomed to peace, has brought forth such new and astounding traits of character, has not yet produced such another marvel as Cleveland—a man whose story will be told around the fireside for an hundred years to come, as one of the most brutal of villains—as one of the most romantic heroes.